W9-ACV-793

Keely.
The city of the dagger.   √ j398.2 (1)
                                    Burma

MT. LEBANON PUBLIC LIBRARY

PLEASE DO NOT REMOVE CARDS FROM
POCKET.
25¢ CHARGE FOR LOSS OF A CARD.
FINES: 5 FOUR CENTS A DAY, INCLUDING
SUNDAYS AND HOLIDAYS UP TO 30 DAYS.
AFTER 30 DAYS THE FINE WILL BE $2.50.
A BORROWER IS RESPONSIBLE FOR BOOKS
DAMAGED OR LOST WHILE CHARGED ON
HIS CARD.

The City of the Dagger

and Other Tales from Burma

ILLUSTRATED BY CHRISTINE PRICE

Frederick Warne and Company, Inc.
New York and London

The City of the Dagger

and Other Tales from Burma

RETOLD BY H. H. KEELY
AND CHRISTINE PRICE

Copyright © H. H. Keely and Christine Price 1971
All Rights Reserved
Library of Congress Catalog Card Number 70-161066
Manufactured in the United States of America
Designed by Joan Maestro

j
398.7
Burma
(1)

MAY 17 '72

MT. LEBANON PUBLIC LIBRARY

Contents

To Burma,
the land of my mother,
this book is dedicated
in joy and gratitude.

H.H.K.

The Storytellers

The Feast of Lights, heralding the end of the Buddhist Lent, is over for another year. After all the fun and excitement the children are bored and restless, and for the fourth time someone calls out: "What shall we do?"

Then the first cool breath of autumn drifts in from the north, and boredom vanishes. Everyone runs about collecting fuel, and soon a wood fire is hissing and crackling under a large *neem* tree.

Fine cane mats are placed over the coarse bamboo ones around the fire, and Mother and two aunts take their seats. Tubes of green bamboo have been cut, filled with rice and water and put on the fire to cook. Chestnuts are ready for roasting, and the earthenware kettle

9

is filled for brewing Shan tea. Finally the youngest child is sent to ask Grandmother to join the others.

Grandmother comes, a small slight person, less than five feet tall. She is temperamental, cross-grained, loving and masterful.

"What story do you want?" she asks as she settles herself on the mat with the children gathered around her.

"We want the one about the crocodile!"

"No, the tiger!"

"The elephant!"

Grandmother raises her finely-shaped hand, and the shouting instantly stops. "I'll tell you the story of the kind-hearted rabbit."

It is like her to choose a story no one had suggested, and as soon as that tale is told, another one begins.

By and by the rice is ready, and the charred bamboo tubes are taken from the fire and peeled as one peels a banana. The long cylinder of sticky rice within, held together by the thin inner skin of the bamboo, is pulled apart into short lengths and munched with a seasoning of chestnuts, pounded sesame seeds and salt. Then everyone sips green tea from the little tea bowls. As Grandmother starts another tale, the white smoke from the fire drifts upward to the bright moon.

Or it is a breathless summer's evening. Fretful and parched with the heat, we are lounging on a large low platform away from the stuffiness of the house. Then Mother begins a story in her quiet, gentle voice: "In the very old days. . . ."

As the tale casts its spell, the prickly heat ceases to prickle, and we forget to make trips to the big earthenware pot for a cool drink of sherbet made of tamarind and molasses.

Or, many years later, I am sitting beside a fire in the house of a village headman, high among the hills near the Ruby Mines.

Under the smoke-blackened thatch roof of the living room the smooth wood floor gleams in the firelight, and there are fine cane mats to sit on. Freshly roasted green tea is thrown into the boiling water in the earthenware kettle. China bowls, half-filled with tea, are handed around the circle of men to give us warmth and a feeling of fellowship.

I am a stranger in the country of the Ruby Mines, and I ask a question that has puzzled me. "How did the Burmese king get possession of the Ruby Mines from the Shan people?"

Several voices answer in unison. "Ask the *saya!*"

Saya means doctor or teacher, and we all turn to the local medicine man, seated with us in the firelit circle. He is an old man, swarthy and beetle-browed, with a black moustache, and like most elders among the Shans he wears his hair long, tied in a knot with a headdress of bright pink silk. The people respect him as an astrologer and a man of letters.

I repeat my question, and soon the dark-faced astrologer is unravelling the tale of the City of the Dagger, with a wealth of detail gathered in years gone by from ancient palm-scripts and old writings on bamboo paper.

Or again, several years later, a sudden rainstorm drives us to take shelter in a hamlet in Upper Chindwin. The people living there are small and primitive, quite different from the Shans and Burmese of nearby villages. I am told they are Htamans. The word immediately brings to mind a host of stories, well known in many other parts of Upper Burma, stories of the ferocious five-toed Htaman tiger.

"Is there any connection between these people and the terrible tiger?" I ask.

Within minutes an old gentleman is ushered into the long low hut where we are sheltering from the rain. We sit on a mat-covered bamboo platform three feet off the ground and listen to the eager and willing voice of the old man repeating the tale he had heard as a boy.

Like him, I recall and tell again some of the stories I was told in Upper Burma long ago.

H. H. K.

The Throne of Tagaung

 1

Paul Kyaing Seeks His Fortune

Long ago in Burma there lived a young man named Pauk Kyaing. His father and mother wished him to be learned and wise, and they sent him far from home to study at the ancient University of Sampannagore. Pauk Kyaing listened hard to the words of his teachers, but he was no student. The ancient learning written in the palm-leaf books meant nothing to him. All his delight was in hunting and swordplay and the show of strength.

When at last his time of learning was over, Pauk Kyaing knelt before his tutor to say farewell, and the old man spoke sadly.

"You are the finest swordsman in Sampannagore, Pauk Kyaing," he said, "but in all my years here, I have never worked so hard, with so little success, to teach a student wisdom. You seem to remember nothing that I tell you! Yet there are three sayings that I would beg you to remember. Keep them ever fresh in your mind, and they will be guides to you and will smooth your way through difficulty and danger.

"Now say after me, Pauk Kyiang:

"A journey ends happily only after much travel.

"Only by much questioning will vital knowledge be gained.

"Less sleep and more wakefulness will insure long life."

Pauk Kyaing obediently learned the three sayings by heart. Then he bowed to receive his tutor's blessing and set off cheerfully on his long journey home, with his few possessions tied up in a bag which hung from the sheathed sword on his shoulder. He repeated the three sayings as he strode along. They were firmly planted in his mind, and he vowed he would never forget them.

He had been walking for many days when he came to a fork in the road. The left branch led to his home,

where he knew his old parents were eagerly awaiting him. Should he take the left and reach home in a week? Or should he take the right and go deep into unknown country? Suddenly he thought of his tutor's first saying: "A journey ends happily only after much travel."

Without hesitation he chose the path to the right.

Two weeks later he looked from the top of a rise across the wooded valley of a river. On the far shore was a steep conical hill, girdled on three sides by the river and crowned by the rooftops of a town and the towers of a wonderful palace.

Pauk Kyaing turned to an old man leaning against a tree beside the path. "What place is that?" he asked.

"That is Tagaung," the old man muttered.

"The palace looks beautiful," said the boy. "Who is the king?"

"There is no king."

"No king?" said Pauk Kyaing. "A splendid city, a beautiful palace and no king? Did the people ever have a king?"

"Of course they had a king. Not one but several kings, one after the other."

The old man seemed so unfriendly that Pauk Kyaing was about to move on. Then he suddenly remembered: "Only by much questioning can vital knowledge be gained."

"Venerable Sir," he said humbly, "I pray you to explain. Why do these people have no king?"

The old man's hard look became more gentle, and he

squatted down beside the path. "Lay down your bundle and rest, young man," he said, "and I will tell you the sad story of this place.

"The first king came here from a far country with all his people—men, women and children with their elephants and horses, goats and cattle. He was a young prince then, not yet crowned, but his people loved him and would have followed him to the end of the earth. Together they had journeyed through jungles and over mountains, seeking a place that the prince had seen in a dream—a steep hill with a river at its foot. Here he found that hill, and here he commanded his people to build the capital city of Tagaung and the royal palace that had appeared on the hilltop of his dream.

"The prince had seen in sleep the towers and windows of his future palace. He had also seen his own great room within, and the mighty king-post, golden, smooth and shining, that supported its roof. Now the royal astrologer told the prince where such a post could be cut, and men and elephants went forth to find the giant tree. Its girth could not be spanned by four men with arms outspread, and when they felled the tree a spring burst forth from the pit beneath it—the spring we call *Tagaung-nan-daing* (The Palace Post of Tagaung).

"The elephants dragged the tree down to the river and heaved it into the water to float downstream to the city. But there was something strange, something evil about that tree. Suddenly it stood on end in the water and would not move. The men were afraid, and the elephants refused to go near the tree. Finally the men thought to make a sacrifice to the spirits that dwelt in the tree—the *nats*—and behold! as soon as the food-offering was raised on high, the tree fell back into the river and floated on.

"So all the way to the city the men made offerings of flowers and fresh-killed wildfowl, betel nuts, tobacco and red cloth, and they garlanded the tree with flowers and fruit and coloured silk. Boatloads of musicians and singers came out to meet the tree, as it neared the city, and the prince himself was waiting to receive it at the landing stage of Tagaung.

"The great tree was built into the new palace as the king-post of the royal bedchamber, and the post was smoothed and polished until it shone. Then came the coronation of the young prince and his wife as King and Queen of Tagaung. Oh, what joy, what laughter and feasting! The beginning of times of good fortune for everyone!"

"But I do not understand, Venerable Sir," said Pauk Kyaing. "You said this would be a sad story!"

"Soon you will understand," said the old man. "On the night of the coronation day, the king left the queen's apartment and went to his room to sleep upon his bed. At dawn the Chamberlain went in to see that all was well. The bedclothes were torn and covered with blood, and on the bed lay the broken body of the king. No trace of his murderer could be found, for no man had killed him. His wounds were made by the teeth of some great beast.

"Ever since that dreadful night, princes and young noblemen have come here from lands far and near, seeking the throne of Tagaung and the hand of the beautiful queen. One by one they have come, and every one of them has met his death on his first night in the royal bedchamber. For a long time now, the throne has been empty and no man has sought it."

As Pauk Kyaing listened, his heart beat faster and his face flushed hot. "How does a man offer himself to be king?" he asked.

"It is easy, fatally easy," said the old man. "He strikes the great gong that hangs outside the eastern gate of the palace and he calls out: 'I have come to be King of Tagaung!' But you would be a fool to try, young man! Do you want to be just another body for the burning? Why should you die so soon, when all life is before you?"

Pauk Kyaing shouldered his sword and bundle. "Thank you, Aged Sir," he said, "and farewell!"

The old man watched him stride down the path to the river and call a boatman to ferry him over to the city; and within the hour the boom of the great gong at the Eastern Gate echoed across the valley.

2

The King's Bedchamber

Darkness had fallen when Pauk Kyaing entered the royal apartment. A servant closed the door behind him and he was alone. No one in the palace had even asked his name, and he had caught not a glimpse of the queen.

Lit by tall beeswax candles and little flickering lamps, the room was the most beautiful he had ever seen. How could it be a place of doom and death?

The mighty king-post gleamed golden with the sheen of satin. A few feet away from it stood the royal bed, magnificent with its spotless linen, soft pillows and embroidered silk cover. Beyond the bed were the doors of the queen's chamber, kept bolted and barred until the royal wedding.

With his naked sword in his hand, Pauk Kyaing forced himself to search the room for hidden dangers. He even peered under the bed, but only darkness was there. Yet the bed worried him, and suddenly he remembered the last saying of his tutor: "Less sleep and more wakefulness will insure long life."

A small door at the end of the room opened into the garden, and this gave Pauk Kyaing an idea. He crept outside and used his sword to cut down a banana tree. He lopped off the stiff, rattling leaves and trimmed the trunk to the height of a man. Then he laid the tree trunk on the bed, pulling up the bedclothes over it. He blew out several candles, and in the dim light the tree under the coverlet looked like a sleeping man.

Pauk Kyaing crawled beneath the bed and lay down to wait. He repeated silently, over and over: "Less sleep and more wakefulness will insure long life."

For hours he lay there, waiting, waiting and fighting against sleep. Then suddenly he heard a hissing sound that sent shivers down his spine. Gripping the sword, he slowly lifted the edge of the bedcover and peered out.

The mighty king-post towered above him. A long gash had opened in the wood, and out of its depths emerged the broad, flattened head of a dragon. The eyes shone red; the forked tongue darted to and fro; and the upper lip drew back to expose a pair of huge curved fangs.

The long hiss came again like exploding steam, and

then the dragon shot out and struck the bed a smashing blow. Pauk Kyaing leaped into the open. The dragon had its fangs buried in the soft banana-trunk, and before it could shake them free, the bright sword rose and fell, chopping the great head from the body. The teeth still gripped the tree trunk, and the headless body thrashed and writhed on the floor. Pauk Kyaing sprang back and watched the body weaken until it lay still at his feet.

"O Dragon, killer of kings," he said, "now death has come to you. For so long you have been a chained spirit, a prisoner in the smooth and shining king-post that once was a mighty forest tree. Now you are released at last. May your new existence lead you to a higher path."

As he spoke, he thought he heard the faint sound of a pagoda drum, acknowledging his prayer for the poor tortured spirit. Yet in that same moment, there was another sound, far beyond his hearing. In the distant village where Pauk Kyaing was born a voice was speaking, loud and clear, to his father and mother while they lay asleep.

"Rise up and go to Tagaung," the voice commanded them. "Your son is at Tagaung, and he has need of you."

 3

The Queen's Test

The Chamberlain and his two assistants walked slowly to the royal bedchamber the next morning, dreading the sight of yet another murdered man. They opened the door, and then they stood amazed.

The bedclothes were torn and rumpled and the blood-stained cover trailed on the floor, but the young man lying on the bed was peacefully asleep. His breathing was gentle and his face serene and glowing with health. Beyond the bed lay the headless body of a dragon, and at the foot of the king-post was the trunk of a banana tree with the dragon's head still clutching it in huge curved fangs.

"The young man lives! The dragon is dead!" cried one of the assistants and ran to spread the news.

The Chief Minister was informed at once, and the arrangements for Pauk Kyaing's funeral and the burning of his body were changed to plans for celebration. The ministers gathered in the Council Chamber, and Pauk Kyaing, dressed in royal garments, was ushered into their presence. But he saw only the beautiful queen, sitting with sad and downcast eyes. He gazed at her in wonder and hardly had strength to take his place beside her on the dais.

Then he heard the voice of the Chief Minister. "Your Highness, we are filled with joy to see you alive and well, and to know that you have lifted the curse from this place and freed us all from the tyranny of the evil spirit. Yet there is one more trial before Your Highness can be crowned King of Tagaung. This is the queen's test, which will prove your fitness to be her lord and king.

"Success in this final test will bring you a royal wedding and a crown; failure, a wretched death on the gallows. What is your desire? You may choose to undergo the test, or you may leave the palace and the city as freely as you came, having earned our everlasting gratitude."

At the last words, Pauk Kyaing met the quick glance of the queen, and her deep blush made her more beautiful than ever. His heart was so full of love for her that he could scarcely speak. "What is the queen's test?" he whispered.

It was the queen herself who answered him. "Proof

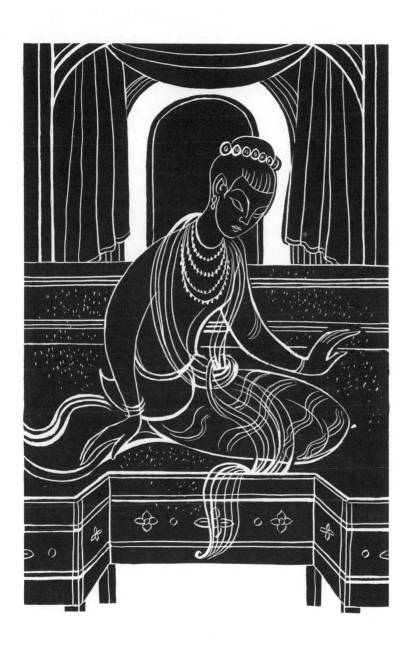

of your courage, strength and determination we already have. Mine will be a test of your mind."

Pauk Kyaing trembled, and for the first time he was afraid.

"I am setting you a riddle," the queen went on. "You have three weeks to find the answer, and the riddle is this: What is it that was torn for a thousand, sewn for a hundred and carved for ten?"

Pauk Kyaing asked for the riddle to be written down, fearing he would forget it otherwise. The Chief Minister wrote the words rapidly on a palm leaf, and Pauk Kyaing left the Council Chamber with the leaf in his hand.

All that day, and the days that came after, he paced to and fro in the royal apartment repeating the riddle over and over again. He had no need of the palm script; the words were burned into his brain. "What is it that was torn for a thousand, sewn for a hundred and carved for ten?" Would the answer never come?

At meals he would stop eating and forget the food, as he repeated the words and started pacing again, and at night he would lie sleepless with the riddle ringing in his ears. None of the sayings he had learned was of any help now, and he blamed the sayings for leading him to this terrible choice: the throne or the gallows.

The first week passed, and the second. The days of the third slid quickly by. Then came the last day of all, and still he had no answer to the queen's riddle.

On the last evening, Pauk Kyaing looked out of a window of the palace and saw the gallows set up outside the town, ready for his hanging. Two black crows were perched on the gallows, and while he watched them, they flew down into the shade of a big banyan tree where a man and a woman were sitting on the ground. The people were eating food from banana leaves. They tossed the scraps to the crows and were leaning back to rest after their meal when suddenly they leaped to their feet.

The crows flew away in alarm, and the two people came running up the hill toward the town, as fast as they could go.

4

The Speech of the Birds

There was a thunderous knocking at the door of the royal apartment, and the voice of a servant called: "Your Highness, Your Highness, there are two old people here who insist on seeing you—they say they are your parents!"

Pauk Kyaing threw open the door. "Let them in!" he commanded, and his parents ran breathless into the room.

He dropped on his knees before them. "My father, my mother! Why are you here? How have you come so far to find me?"

"My son, my son!" cried his father. "We were summoned here by a voice in a dream. Both of us heard it, loud and clear, telling us to come to Tagaung, for you were here and had need of us. O my son! Is it true that you are to be hanged tomorrow? I beg you to tell us it is not true!"

Pauk Kyaing bowed his head. "Father, it is true indeed—I would that you did not know! Who has told you this thing? Who has told you of my shame?"

"We listened to the speech of the crows that ate the scraps from our meal, out yonder near the gallows. They spoke your name and said you were to die. But why is this, my son? They said you had bravely killed a dragon and freed the kingdom from a curse, that you had won the right to be king and to marry the beautiful queen. But then we did not understand—they seemed to speak in riddles—"

"In *riddles!*" Pauk Kyaing stared at his father. "Oh, father, I beg of you, what was the riddle that they spoke?"

"Something about tens and thousands—I know not!"

"I remember it," cried the old mother through her tears. "They said a man had skinned the dragon that you killed, and he was paid a thousand ticals of silver for his work; and a woman cut and sewed the skin to make a cushion for the royal throne, and she received a hundred ticals; and an ivory-carver took the fangs of the dragon and made them into hairpins for the queen, and his fee was ten ticals—"

Pauk Kyaing leaped into the air. His parents gazed at him as though he were mad. He called in servants to take care of the old people, to bring them fresh clothes and the finest food and drink. Trembling from head to foot, he adjusted his silken turban, washed face and hands and prayed his parents to excuse him and await his return. Then he went forth to find the queen.

Darkness had fallen, and the tall wax candles were lit in the Council Chamber where the queen received him in the presence of the ministers. She sat on her throne, still as a carven image.

"It is the end of the last day," she said in a low voice, and she repeated the words of the riddle: "What is it that was torn for a thousand, sewn for a hundred and carved for ten?"

"O my queen," he answered, bowing deeply before the throne, "the answer lies in the body of the dead dragon. For a thousand ticals it was skinned; for a hundred the skin was stitched to make a cushion for the royal throne; and for ten the cruel fangs were carved to make wonderful ivory hairpins for your lovely hair."

A great sigh of relief arose from the people in the room, for all would have grieved to see the brave Pauk Kyaing put to death. But Pauk Kyaing saw only the queen, her eyes filled with tears of joy, and heard only her sweet voice, as she held out her hand to him. "Come, take your seat beside me, O my king!"

The celebrations for the royal wedding and coronation were the finest ever seen in Tagaung. The whole city rang with music, night and day. Glittering processions wound their way through the streets, and the people rejoiced with songs and dances and feasting. The parents of Pauk Kyaing were guests of honour, loaded with gifts, dressed in the loveliest silks and given the choicest food at all the feasts.

Pauk Kyaing would never forget that his father and mother had saved his life. He told the queen what they had done for him, and she too loved the old couple and wanted them to stay forever at the palace. But they were homesick for the quietness of their village.

It was the simple goodness of their lives that had given Pauk Kyaing's parents their understanding of the speech of birds and beasts. They were afraid that in the gaiety of life at court their ears would become dulled and their understanding of wild creatures would be lost.

So Pauk Kyaing and the queen said farewell to them with sadness, and watched them ride away on an elephant with a retinue of servants for protection.

When the travellers had disappeared into the forest beyond the river, Pauk Kyaing turned to the queen. "From this same window I looked out at the gallows where I was to hang," he said. "Yet I do not believe I was afraid to die. What pierced my heart was the thought of losing you."

"Do you think I would have let you die?" she said. "If your parents had not come to help you on the last day, I was prepared to solve the riddle for you late that night."

Pauk Kyaing's eyes glowed with happiness. "Why should you have done that for me, my queen?" he asked.

"Because you were too strong and brave to be allowed to die," she answered. "And I—and all the people of Tagaung—needed you to reign as our king."

And Pauk Kyaing proved to be a good king. He reigned in prosperity and peace, and he was loved and honored by the people of that first Burmese kingdom.

The Fate of the Two Princes

 1

King Pauk Kyaing had ruled Tagaung wisely and well for many years. His kingdom prospered and his people should have been happy. But they were sorely troubled.

The queen had borne no children.

"All of us are mortal," the people said. "The king cannot live forever, and if he dies and leaves no heir, we shall once again be without a ruler."

Men recalled the terrible time, before the coming of Pauk Kyaing, when Tagaung had had no king. All who mounted the throne and sought the hand of the queen had died horrible and mysterious deaths. Although Pauk Kyaing had slain the dragon, the killer of the kings, the people were still full of fears. If Pauk Kyaing died without an heir, some new monster might rise up to prey upon the kingdom, and Tagaung would fall once more into decay and ruin.

Some people said the King should take another wife; others declared that the beautiful queen should not be so cruelly humiliated. The king would be wiser, they said, if he adopted an able young man to be his heir.

The Prime Minister, the Town Governor and the high officials and nobles of the court wracked their brains in vain to find a solution to the problem. Finally it was a Man in the Street, an ordinary townsman of Tagaung, who decided what must be done.

In the main thoroughfares and busy marketplaces of the town he called upon the people to hear him. "Good people, listen!" he shouted. "We must all pray to the spirits to give the queen a son! Next Friday, let all of us make offerings to the *nats*. Do this every Friday, good people! Present the richest offerings you can afford! The *nats* will be unable to withstand the pressure of your prayers; they will be forced to help us!"

Even in those ancient days the will of the united people could not be denied by men or *nats*. Before the tenth Friday had passed by, the people knew that the *nats* had responded to their prayers. The queen was to have a child.

At once the queen's health became the concern of the whole kingdom. People talked endlessly of her headaches, her sudden fancy to eat chalk or charcoal, her bursts of energy or days of lassitude. Courtiers and palace servants were beseiged with questions about the queen until at last the astonishing news was announced. Not one but two sons had been born!

The people danced in the streets in a frenzy of delight. "Two sons," they cried, "when we asked for one! Truly the *nats* have been good to us!"

Few stopped to think that the spirits had acted unwillingly, only after the people's constant prayers had broken down their resistance. Soon strange rumours began to filter into the city from the palace. It seemed that all was not well with the little princes. At first there were only hints and whisperings; then the awful truth could be hidden no longer. The twin princes had been born blind.

The kingdom was plunged into gloom. Neither prince could be heir to the throne, for according to tradition no blind man could be crowned king. Worse still, the twins should not be allowed to live. Since ancient times a royal baby with any serious physical blemish was killed at birth. Yet the two little princes had been born with beautiful eyes, and no one suspected then that they were blind.

The boys were now a year old. All who had seen them said how handsome, happy and strong they were and how dearly their parents loved them. No more was said about their blindness. The twins grew up to be six years old, and then the queen had another son—a child without blemish or defect.

"Tradition should be obeyed, or trouble will come," said the old folk of the town. "The twins should be killed so that the new babe may be heir to the throne."

Yet still the twins were allowed to live. The three princes played together, and the two blind ones, Maha Thanbawa and Sula Thanbawa, were always gay and full of laughter. They moved about the palace and the gardens as nimbly as though they could see. They knew their world so well by sound and smell and touch that they could be taught everything a prince should learn, even the use of arms. The two princes never thought of themselves as different from their brother until at last a day came when their lives were changed forever.

MT. LEBANON PUBLIC LIBRARY

 2

On that fateful day Maha and Sula were almost eighteen years old. They were walking in the palace garden in the coolness of early morning, enjoying the birdsong and the fragrance of flowers, when they heard the voice of their old friend, the head gardener. He was talking to someone in a tone of such urgency that the boys stopped to listen.

"The king is a very worried man of late," the gardener was saying. "I have never seen him so unhappy."

"What is troubling him?" asked the shrill voice of the gardener's wife.

"The problem of the twin princes, of course! Now that they are almost grown men, the king must decide what is to be done about them."

"He has waited all these years," said the wife. "Can't he wait until the youngest prince is eighteen and comes of age?"

"There can be no more delay! The decision must be

made when Prince Maha, as the firstborn twin, is eigh-
teen. As tradition forbids us to have a blind Crown
Prince, Prince Maha—must go. And the fate of Prince
Sula will be the same."

"Where must they go?" asked the woman.

"Don't ask foolish questions!" said her husband.

The princes heard the man's footsteps hurrying down
the garden path, and presently the wife went into her
house and slammed the door. Then the only sounds in
the garden were the rustle of leaves and the piping of
the birds.

"So we must go," said Sula at last, as though the
words were hard to speak. "Are we like those princes
we learned about in history? The ones who were born
crippled or deformed and were—"

"Killed," said Maha. "Yes, Sula, we are like them—
unfit to rule."

"But Father loves us. He would not—"

"He has no choice," said Maha. "He must do what is
right for the kingdom. Do you think it is always easy
and pleasant to be a king? Our parents have suffered
much for our sakes, Sula, and I think they have loved
us all the more because we cannot see. Now is the time
for us to repay them for their love."

Maha took his brother by the hand and explained to
him in whispers what they must do. Then they moved
swiftly along the path through the garden to the palace.

A servant opened the golden doors for the princes to
enter and led them to the queen. She was sitting in a

small room that overlooked the garden, and at the sight
of her two sons with stern and serious faces she asked
them laughingly what was the matter.

"We would speak with you and Father," said Sula.

When the king had joined them and dismissed the
servants, the princes knelt before their parents and
Maha spoke. "Sula and I are no longer children; we are
nearing man's estate. We must leave Tagaung."

"What? You want to leave us?" exclaimed the queen.

"We do not want to, but we must," answered Maha,
staring at her with his sightless eyes. "We have no
choice. We must make our own way. We must leave before we come of age, and time is short!"

"And what are your reasons for leaving?" the king
demanded.

Sula answered for both of them. "We have been a
burden to you in the past, and if we stay we shall be a
greater burden. We are useless to you. Neither of us
can be heir to the throne. For the sake of the people and
the kingdom we must go. Our brother will be Crown
Prince, and we refuse to be a trouble to you or to him."

"We might have fled without telling you," said Maha,
"but we could not bear to go away without your blessing. And we need your help, Father, in planning our escape. Whether we go by water or by land, we must leave
quietly; we must not upset the people."

Pauk Kyaing went over to the window and looked out
past the gardens to the shining water of the Irrawaddy
River, far below the palace and the town.

"You have spoken bravely and wisely, my sons," he said. "Your words prove to us what worthy sons we have. Speak of this matter to no one else. Whatever is done must be done in secret."

True to the king's desire, no announcement was made about the princes' decision. Not even a rumour reached the ears of the townspeople, and few men in the palace knew what was afoot. One of them was the head gardener, the princes' friend.

In his youth the gardener had been a boatman on the Irrawaddy, and it was he who supervized the preparations for the princes' going. Under his watchful eye, the palace carpenters began to build a large raft.

It was no ordinary raft made of lengths of thin bamboo. Only the giant bamboo called *wabo* was used, each hollow stem as thick as a man's leg and fit to keep the raft afloat for years. Beams of teakwood were laid along the sides for extra strength. A roomy hut for shelter was built amidships, with roof and walls of matting, and astern there was a long steering oar.

Before the raft was finished the princes were learning the skills of river boatmen. The gardener showed them how to lean against the steering oar and how to judge direction by the changing breath of the wind in their faces. He took them on secret journeys down the river by dugout canoe. They learned to feel the river's current beneath their craft, to listen for the sound of water in the shallows and to recognize the smells of trees and underbrush along the shore.

"Even if you run aground or hit a rock," said the old man, "have no fear! Your raft is far too strong to break!"

The gardener was one of the last to see the princes on the night of their going. It was an auspicious night, decided on by the court astrologer. The moon was high, and under the overhanging trees the river lay like black silk threaded with silver. The twins parted from their parents and their young brother in the palace, and a small company of men escorted them down through the gardens to the shore. The gardener was waiting by the raft, and there were tears in his voice as he spoke his farewell. The princes stepped aboard, and servants pushed the raft into the current.

Then the brothers leaned on the steering oar and felt the raft respond to their will. The pain of parting was behind them, and ahead was their unknown destiny. They faced it unafraid.

3

For seven days the princes travelled down the great river. In the daytime they steered the raft by turns. At night they slept and drifted with the current.

Then on the eighth morning they awoke to find the raft was motionless. They scrambled out of their hut and collided with the branch of a great tree. All about them was a thicket of leaves. Yet soundings with a long pole showed them that the raft was in deep water, not aground on a bank.

The boys pushed hard against the branches of the tree, then tried to chop through them with their long knives called *dahs*. But still the raft refused to move.

Finally they agreed to rest and eat, and sitting down under the canopy of leaves they opened a packet of food and placed it between them. They had hardly taken a mouthful of rice when they heard a rustling in the tree and the food was gone.

"You have eaten very quickly, Sula!" said Maha.

"I was about to say the same of you!" said Sula.

Soon a second packet of food lay open between them, but this time they were on their guard. Instead of picking up the food they let their hands hover over it. When the leaves rustled, Maha made a grab and clutched the warm flesh of an arm.

"You thief!" he shouted and drew his long double-edged dagger.

There was a sobbing wail of fear, and Sula exclaimed: "It's a woman!"

"Please do not kill me, Noble Sir," said a soft pleading voice. "I am not a woman but an ogress. I am nursing my twin babies and starving with hunger. Your food smelled so good—I had to steal some! Please have pity on me. I will do anything for you if you will spare my life."

"Anything?" said Maha. "Ogress, or whosoever you are, can you cure us of our blindness?"

"I can indeed," she said, "if you will have patience, and if you will carry me and my sons on your raft."

"Where are your sons?" asked Sula.

"I left them at the top of the tree that has caught your raft in its branches. The tree grows upon a small rocky islet where I took refuge with my little ones."

The brothers agreed to let her fetch the babies, and she vowed she would not try to escape. "You caught me stealing," she said, "and I shall be in your power until I have redeemed my promise to cure your blindness."

When the two babies were safely aboard the raft, the ogress was allowed to go ashore to collect herbs. These she compounded with her milk, and at nightfall she administered four drops of the medicine to each prince— two drops in the right eye and two in the left.

The princes shut their strange companion in the hut with her babies and lay down to sleep outside the door. At first the medicine seemed to have no effect, but when they opened their eyes in the morning, the black night of their blindness was veiled in shimmering grey.

"It must be light!" cried Sula. "The faintest ghost of light!"

When they had shared their morning meal with the ogress, the princes took out their *dahs* and attacked the tree again, trying to free the raft. But the ogress, diving over the side, discovered a rotten branch that clutched the raft from underneath. She borrowed a knife to chop it away, and the raft slid free.

Now, as they journeyed on downstream, the princes received the medicine for their eyes each day at sunset. By the fifth morning they seemed to be in a world of moving shadows; and on the ninth evening the clumsy shape of their companion was quite clear to them, though still they could not see her face.

"Tomorrow," she said, "your eyes will be completely cured. I beg you to let me go my way tonight. It might harm your new-found sight if you were to see my face!"

Sula wanted her to stay until morning, to make certain of the cure, but Maha said: "We trust you, and we know you speak the truth. Go when you will and take all the food you can. Soon we shall be able to find our own food! We were but half men when you came to us; tomorrow we shall be whole."

Under her guidance Maha steered the raft to the shore and it came gently to rest on a shelving beach of sand. "We can never forget you," he said. "All our blessings go with you."

The two princes did not see the tears in the eyes of the ogress nor the wonderful change that came over her as Maha spoke. The small pointed tusks dropped from her ugly mouth; her face became beautiful and her ungainly body took the shape of a lovely young woman. In the hut where she had left her children she found two human babies instead of the wizened little creatures she had known before. She caught them up in her arms, and with the bag of food on her shoulder, she stepped ashore.

"I am redeemed at last," she sobbed. "Farewell, young sirs, and thank you with all my heart!"

The brothers could hardly bear to close their eyes that night. They were awake and out of the hut at the first light of dawn, and there before them was all the world to see.

They saw the river, wide and calm and lovely under the great pale sky. They saw the soft green trees along the banks, the blossoms red and white, the herons feeding in the shallows and the crows that flapped above on broad black wings. And for the first time they saw each other, strong and beautiful, and they laughed aloud for joy.

When the sun rose in a blaze of saffron with silken scarves of cloud in many colours, they were drunk with the glory of it. They scooped up water in their hands for the sheer delight of seeing it fall in drops like sparkling gems.

It was a long time before they could think of food or consider what they should do. When at last they sat down to eat, Sula spoke the thought that was in both their hearts. "Should we return to Tagaung and tell them our glad news?"

Maha paused before he answered. "No, we must go on. Have you forgotten we are now eighteen years old? Father will have told his ministers and his people that we have left Tagaung forever and that our brother will be Crown Prince when he comes of age. It is not for us to return and claim our place as Father's heirs. All that has happened shows that our future does not lie in Tagaung. The river will show us the way."

Sula stared at the mighty river that carried them onward. "You are right," he said. "We must go forward. There can be no turning back."

🌱 4

Now the days were too short for all that the brothers wanted to do. They could go ashore to explore and hunt for food. They could swim, fish or simply sit in the sun, delighting in what they saw. Day by day the raft carried them past places that would be famous cities in years to come—Mandalay, Ava, Amarapura and Pagan. The country along the river changed to a dry wilderness of rocky cliffs, open forest and scrub land; and one day, weary of travelling, they tied the raft to a huge *koko* tree and went ashore.

The land rose, clothed in thin woods, and from a hill-top they saw below them a little lake that shone silver in the sun. A game trail led them down to the lakeside where a slender figure stood among the water lilies.

Maha came to a sudden halt. "It that a *nat-thami?*" he whispered. "Is it spirit or human being?"

They approached without a sound, but the girl sensed their presence and turned to look at them, her eyes round with wonder.

For a moment Maha could only gaze at her. "Beautiful maid," he said at last, "whether you are spirit or human being, what are you doing in this lonely place?"

"I am filling this gourd with water," she replied. "My uncle set me the task and it will take me till sunset."

"Till *sunset*—to fill one gourd?"

Maha gently took the gourd which had only a pinhole to let in the water. He enlarged the hole with a stab and twist of his dagger and handed back the gourd to the girl. As soon as she dipped it in the lake the water gurgled in and filled it to the brim.

"I thank you, kind sir," she said, laughing with delight. "Will you come home with me and see my uncle?"

She led the two princes along a well-worn path through the woods to a small thatched house on stilts in a clearing. "Here are two strangers, Uncle!" she called.

"Come in, young men," said a voice from the house.

The princes climbed the ladder and found an old man in a dark brown robe seated on a mat. He smiled upon them and bade them sit down and rest. "I have waited a long time for this day," he said. "I almost gave up hope of your coming. And now I see not the one prince I expected but two!"

"But how could you be expecting us?" asked Sula. "And how do you know we are princes?"

The old hermit smiled. "Much is revealed to those who meditate and study," he said.

"But Venerable Sir," said Maha, "I beg you to explain. To find you here in this wild jungle is strange enough, but what of the lovely girl, your niece? Are you truly humans—or perhaps spirits in human form?"

"We are not spirits that make sport of you," said the old man. "I have renounced the world and dwelt in this wilderness since my youth—more years than I can tell. But it was only fifteen years ago that the maiden came. I remember well that day. I was gathering my food of fruits and nuts and leaves when I heard the cry of a newborn babe. I found the tiny child alone beside the lake without even a human footprint on the muddy shore. The only other living thing I saw was a deer—a large doe of wondrous grace and beauty.

"The doe departed, as though loath to go. The baby's cries were growing weaker and she needed food. So I carried her home. I named her after the water lilies of the lake—Ma Beda."

"And she has lived with you ever since?" asked Maha.

"She has never left me," said the hermit. "I still have friends in the world I left so long ago, and these old men and women have brought clothes and food for the child. Ma Beda had never seen young people before she saw you today."

"Ma Beda is the first girl we have ever seen," said Maha, gazing at her, "for we were blind. . . ."

"But Venerable Sir," said Sula, "I do not understand! Why did you give Ma Beda a hopeless task to do? The gourd with the tiny hole—"

The hermit laughed softly. "Filling the gourd was merely a device to keep her busy by the lake. I knew by her horoscope and by the stars that this day she would be found by a prince."

Suddenly the hermit's voice took on a tone of authority. "This is also a fateful day for you, young sirs, and you must tarry here no longer. Arise now and return to the place where you came ashore!"

"Oh, Uncle," said Ma Beda. "Do not send them away!"

"Their destiny awaits them, my child," said the old man. "Fear not—they will return!"

"But the hour is early," said Maha, with his eyes on the girl. "If we could stay a little longer—"

"Be well advised, young prince," said the hermit. "Go now before it is too late. My blessing be upon you!"

Maha muttered his farewell and stumbled away with Sula at his heels. Each step he took seemed to Maha an agony. His heart cried out for Ma Beda. He began to wish he had never seen her. How could he have known that the gift of sight could bring such bitter pain?

When they reached the raft, Maha sat down and hid his face in his hands, trying to shut out the vision of the girl. Sula could see his brother's misery and crouched beside him in silence until suddenly the evening stillness was broken by a strange murmur of sound.

Faint at first, but growing louder and clearer, were the voices of many people, the squeak and groan of carts and the neighing of horses. The brothers looked up and turned in the direction of the sound. Then, around the bend of the riverbank, came a long procession of oxcarts and horsemen and people on foot. The sunshine gleamed on swaying silken umbrellas, bright clothes of pink and blue and gold, and weapons and harness trimmed with silver. The two princes sat spellbound and trembling with excitement.

Sula was the first to find his voice. "Look, Maha!" he cried. "The first cart has no one in it, while the others are full of people. The young bulls that draw the empty cart have no rope through their nostrils and no man to guide them! Is that not strange?"

Maha gripped him by the arm. "They seek a king," he whispered. "Don't you remember what our old teacher taught us long ago? He said that when a kingdom was without a king, this was the old, old way to find one. The people would send out a cart with no man to drive it, and under the guidance of the *nats*, the cart would find a man who would be king."

Suddenly Maha rose to his feet and stood still, his tall figure gilded by the setting sun. The empty cart had reached the great *koko* tree; the bulls turned to face the river, walked down to the raft at the water's edge and came to a halt. A mighty shout burst from the crowd: "Behold! Our king! Our king!"

People came pouring down the river bank, and a horseman, battling through the throng, dismounted and bowed low at Maha's feet. "O king!" he exclaimed. "May your reign be glorious!"

Thus Maha Thanbawa was made King of Prome, with the beautiful Ma Beda as his queen and his brother Sula as Commander-in-Chief. There was great joy in Prome at Maha's crowning, but who can describe the joy and thankfulness at Tagaung when messengers brought the glad news of the exiled princes?

Yet in the universal happiness the Man in the Street was forgotten. No one gave a thought to the townsman of Tagaung who had called upon the people to make offerings to the *nats* before the twin princes were born. He saw the work of the *nats* in all that had happened since then, from the birth of the blind princes to the finding of their new kingdom; but it was he who had set in motion these wonderful events.

Whenever he heard news of the strong and prosperous kingdom of Prome and its wise king, Maha Thanbawa, he would glow with pride. He cared not if the people ignored him. He had played a great part in the destiny of kings.

The Htaman Tiger

Of all tigers, large and small, the Htaman Tiger is the most ferocious, most wily and most cunning. It differs from all other tigers for when the Htaman Tiger walks abroad, its great feet leave pug-marks with five toes instead of four. It has not the slightest fear of man, and the village people say that when the spirits are out to punish evildoers, they ride upon the back of a Htaman Tiger.

Such a strange animal as this tiger had a strange beginning, and this is how it happened. . . .

Once there was a terrible storm in the country of the Htaman tribe. The wind howled and roared; the rain poured down in a solid mass, and for a whole week, the

lightning and thunder never ceased. The tribe had never seen anything like it. The Chindwin River had risen forty feet and was still rising. The huts of the Htaman village were sodden with rain; some had been blown clean away.

Then, late on the seventh night of the storm, the tribe was awakened by the father of all earthquakes. With the frightful heaving of the earth, the course of the river was changed and a mighty wave of water swept into the village. The people had barely time to snatch up their children and race for the top of the hill before the village and everything they owned were swallowed up in the flood.

That night, the storm blew itself out, but the next morning, when the sun rose in glory, there was water everywhere. Not the smallest trace remained of houses or boats, animals, chickens or household goods, and the people had not a scrap of food to eat.

When they managed to light a fire, there was nothing to cook. They tried to catch fish, but the fish seemed to have been swept away. The men could not hunt without weapons or dogs. Even the wise elders of the village could think of nothing to do. They sat around the fire and talked and muttered until at last the headman raised his voice.

"There seems to be no way out," he said. "We have not even a chicken or a bull to sacrifice to the *nats*—the good spirits—to beg them for their help. But now I remember—long ago—seeing my grandmother holding a bunch of fresh flowers in her hands while she knelt and prayed to the Great White Spirit. Perhaps we could do the same."

The old men around the fire grunted and muttered their agreement.

"I will go then," the headman said, "and find flowers for the sacrifice."

He hurried away to the forest, halfway up the next mountain, and soon was hidden from their sight.

It was well after midnight—the time of the first cock-crow if the roosters had been alive—when the headman came running back to his people on the hilltop. Quivering with excitement, he called the elders to one side and spoke to them in a rapid whisper.

"We are saved! Listen! I walked for a long time, but no flower could I find. I went deeper into the forest than I had ever been before, and I was ready to turn back when suddenly I broke into a clearing and saw there a bush covered with small white flowers of wonderful scent. I gathered nine sprigs, for my grandmother said nine was a mystic number. Then I raised the flowers to the sky and said: 'O Great White Spirit, worshipped by my granny, listen to us. We are destitute. We are hungry and likely to die. Save us. Help us.'

"Then I sat down near the bush of flowers and fell into a deep sleep. I awoke to hear a voice saying: 'O Htaman Headman, take heart. Your people shall be saved. Return and instruct the nine elders as I shall instruct you now. Then tonight and for many nights to

come, the ten of you will be able to provide food for
your people. Each one of you, before he dies, must pass
on these instructions to his eldest son. No one else must
ever know the secret.'

"And now," said the headman, gathering the elders
close about him, "listen very carefully. This is what the
spirit told me that we must do."

The headman spoke for a long time in a low whisper;
then he and the nine elders left the fireside, two by two,
and made for the forest. The people stared after them,
wondering what they would do, but before the morning was gone, they knew!

The elders came staggering back with great loads of
fresh venison, enough and to spare for everyone in the
starving tribe. What a feast there was! How greedily
and noisily and happily everyone ate that meal of wonderful meat! Hunger and weariness were gone; the people were up and doing. Plans were made to build a
bigger and better village, high on the hill where they
had lit the first fire after the flood.

The tribe grew stronger and healthier on a diet of
meat, and soon the elders no longer needed to find food
for the people. The men could go hunting for themselves. Everyone was ready to forget their sufferings and
their narrow escape from death.

But the elders knew that the help of the Great White
Spirit must never be forgotten. They decided that on
the anniversary of the headman's prayer to the Spirit,
and each year thereafter, the original ten men should

go in solemn procession to the forest clearing to give thanks and to make a promise never to use the Spirit's wonderful gift except in time of dire necessity.

Now it happened that one of the nine elders was very ill and was not expected to live. His house in the village was deathly quiet, and everyone in his family spoke in whispers—except for his youngest son, Ai Hsam. He was eleven years old and could never keep quiet for long. Even with his father gravely ill, Ai Hsam managed to sing and shout and knock over pots and pans with a mighty clatter. His eldest brother had just smacked him for making a noise, when his mother, with tears in her eyes, told the eldest son to go to his father.

Hearing that, young Ai Hsam felt unwanted and lonely. He slipped away into the shadows under the house, which stood on tall posts like all the other village houses. What could his sick father be telling the eldest son? Suddenly Ai Hsam was afire with curiosity. He shinnied up a post of the house until he was just under the floor where his father lay and then he heard his father speak.

"My son, you must tell this to no one until the time of your death, when you will pass on to *your* eldest son what I shall tell you now. Once a year you will be summoned to thank the Great White Spirit, but the strange power that I shall tell you of must never be used unless it is vital for the good of the village."

The father's voice dropped very low, but Ai Hsam, crouching under the floor, heard every word and stored it up as though his life depended on it. When he heard his brother repeating the instructions, Ai Hsam ran off in search of his best friend, Ai Lu; for only with the help of a companion could he do what he planned to do.

Late that evening, the two boys approached a large tree standing by itself in a small clearing of the forest. While Ai Hsam took off his cotton skirt, which was all he had on, and folded it at the foot of the tree, Ai Lu climbed the tree and straddled the first branch.

"Are you ready?" he called down.

"Yes, I'm ready. Hurry up!" said Ai Hsam.

Then Ai Lu closed his eyes and chanted:

> *"Go forth and slay the noble stag,*
> *"Return with it to this place.*
> *"Never falter, fear nor delay;*
> *"The Great White Spirit commands;*
> *"Oom Padama, Oom Dwiya, Oom Phwat—GO!"*

At the word "Go" Ai Hsam turned into a mighty tiger! Ai Lu was frozen with horror. The tiger leaped into the air and playfully clawed at him. When it cantered away with a loud roar, the boy fainted and fell out of the tree. As soon as he came to himself, he sprang to his feet and ran for the village as he had never run before.

Presently the tiger returned to the clearing with a fresh-killed stag, placed it at the foot of the tree and waited. There was his cotton skirt, but where was Ai

Lu? Ai Hsam had enjoyed being a tiger, but now he wanted to be a boy again and go home. Perhaps Ai Lu should be reminded of his duty. Ai Hsam ran off down the hill and made straight for his friend's house, calling "Ai Lu! Ai Lu!" But his calls were loud roars.

As he neared the village, sticks and stones greeted him and arrows missed him by inches. When a well-aimed spear grazed his shoulder, he somersaulted backwards and fled into the forest.

He waited by the tree all night and half the next day, until his hunger was so great he bit into the haunch of the deer. The raw flesh tasted very good—the best thing he had ever eaten. He made a full heavy meal, then dragged the stag under some bushes, drank at a stream and slept the sleep of a sated tiger. When he awoke, he was a tiger, through and through, and no more a little boy.

Soon a new tiger, which left five-toed pug-marks, was hunting in the forest on the mountain. The human blood in his veins made him the most ferocious, the most cunning and wily of tigers, without the slightest fear of man. Only spirits could put fear into the heart of the Htaman Tiger, for the boy Ai Hsam had offended the Great White Spirit. He was bound forever to serve as a steed for angry spirits out to punish evildoers.

Ai Hsam was the first of the Htaman Tigers, and all his descendants after him, from that day to this, have been feared and respected as the most powerful, and most terrible, of all the tiger tribe.

The Heir of Thaton

1

In a palace on the shore of India the exiled Queen of Thaton looked eastward over the sea. A ship was moored at the quay below her window, proud and beautiful as a great bird ready to take wing. The queen turned from the window with tears in her eyes, and suddenly the door of her room flew open. Her son, Prince Zanekka, strode across the carpeted floor and fell on his knees at her feet.

"Oh my mother!" he cried. "My ship is ready at last! A

picked crew is waiting, and my five hundred companions are aboard. The tide is turning and the wind is fair. Mother I beg you to give your consent and your blessing to our mission!"

The prince looked up into his mother's face, marked by lines of sorrow and pain. She moved away from him to hide her tears and sat down wearily on the carpet by the door.

"I have seen your ship, my son," she said in a low voice, "but how can I bless your venture when it will bring death to you and to the finest young men in the land? I have lost my husband; must I also lose my son?"

"But Mother, we cannot fail!" said the prince, kneeling again before her. "You know how long and carefully we have prepared for this day. And now, across the sea, victory awaits us!"

"You do not know, my son," said the queen, "what dangers lie ahead. Your uncle was a mighty warrior and leader of men when he deposed and slew your father and seized for himself the kingdom of Thaton. Even your father, with all his wisdom, was no match for him. And now, with five hundred men of your own age— barely nineteen years—you plan to land on that hostile shore and challenge your uncle, the all-powerful King of Thaton!"

"But he is all-powerful no longer!"

Zanekka's words burst out in an angry torrent. "My uncle may have been strong when he killed my father, but now he is a broken man, tortured by sleepless,

haunted nights and days of pain. His rule grows harsher day by day, for he lives in terror of the people—*our* people! They can never forget his murdered brother, the wise good king. Our spies have told us how the people long to rise up against their false ruler, and how they long for me, the rightful heir of Thaton, to return from over the sea!"

Zanekka stretched out his hands to the queen and tried to speak more calmly. "Oh my mother, I was a child when we fled to safety, here in your father's kingdom. Now I am a man, and I must claim the throne that is mine by right. My people are waiting for me, and they will rise, as one, to help me overthrow my uncle."

"How can you be so sure, my son?" said the queen with bitterness. "The tales of spies must be weighed in the balance; too often they are worthless! Remember this also, my son: as we have spies in Thaton, so your uncle has spies here, who can tell him of your mission. If you ever reach Thaton, he will be well prepared for your coming. But first you must cross the wide sea, such a cruel and stormy sea at this time of year—"

She gazed at the prince, and her voice was soft and pleading. "Wait a while with your mother, Zanekka. Your uncle is not immortal. Let him die, and then let the people invite you to return."

He answered her gently, choosing his words with care. "There can be no waiting, Mother. My uncle may live for many years. Not only must I avenge my father's death and your widowhood, but the people have a right to be freed from this tyrant. Please let me go. I make my obeisance in farewell."

Still kneeling, he put his open palms together. Then with forefingers touching his brow, he bent down to the floor three times in the old gesture of leave-taking.

The mother's voice changed. "No, you shall not go! My precious son, you are all I have. I will not let you go!"

The misery in her broken voice pierced him with a stab of pain. He hesitated for a moment, and a gleam of hope lit the queen's face. She sat with her legs outstretched on the carpet, barring the way to the door. He would have to step over them to leave the room, an act of great disrespect.

If I go, I shall have to suffer for this act, he thought. But it was too late now to give in.

He stood up. Begging his mother's forgiveness, he stepped over her outstretched legs and passed through the doorway. His heart was torn by her last despairing cry: "O my son, do not leave me!" But when he reached the dockside and saw his ship, he was fired again with all the glory of his mission.

The masts of the ship towered above him, with sailors busy in the rigging. His five hundred followers were assembled to greet him, and the ship's captain was waiting for orders. The prince sprang onto the poop deck between the two great steering oars that would hold the ship on her eastward course.

"Forward!" he shouted. "Forward to Thaton—and victory!"

MT. LEBANON PUBLIC LIBRARY

 2

Six nights later the prince's ship, under full sail, was dipping and rolling through dark, foamless seas. At the start of the voyage the vessel had seemed sluggish, loath to leave the land. Now she was speeding onward under the stars with the song of the wind in her rigging.

Prince Zanekka stood on the poop deck and thought of the awesome task that lay ahead of him. Suddenly he heard the gruff voice of old Appana, the mate.

"I don't like the look of that yellow ring around the sickle moon," Appana said. "It's only two days since the first quarter. The last time I saw such a ring we were shipwrecked."

"There is nothing to fear," said an old sailor named Kalinga. "The time of danger comes two days before and two days after the *full* moon, not the first quarter."

"Will we not be near Thaton by then?" asked the prince.

"We will indeed, Your Excellency," said Kalinga, "if this wind holds."

"The wind is rising too fast," said Appana, "and look there!"

He pointed to the southwest where a black cloud was blotting out the stars. Even while they watched and listened, the singing of the wind changed to a shriek, and the masts began to swing in widening arcs against the sky. The mounting waves were crested with foam, blown out in long tatters by the wind.

The mate ran to warn the captain who was sleeping below, and men swarmed aloft to shorten sail. Then, with the fury of a thousand demons, the storm struck.

The ship heeled over and fled before the onslaught. Mighty waves broke over her decks with a terrible crashing. The men at the steering oars were swept into the boiling cauldron of the sea, and the waters hammered the unmanned oars and tore them away. Without her steersmen, the ship reeled and staggered, helpless under the battering of the sea. Two of the three masts were snapped like reed-stems and hurled into the water, with men still clinging to spars and rigging. Prince Zanekka and a handful of others had lashed themselves to the last remaining mast, and all night they hung there, half drowned, flung to and fro, up and down, in a nightmare world of wild water and yelling wind.

When at last the storm began to die down, the pale

dawn light revealed a scene of horror. The ship was encircled by dead and dying men at the mercy of a shoal of sharks in the turbulent, blood-stained sea.

Prince Zanekka looked at the poor remnants of his once-proud band, no more than twenty men beside him at the mast. He tried to shout above the din of waves and wind, but his voice was like the cry of a child. "We cannot stay here. Soon the ship will sink and drag us to our death. The sharks are too close to let us dive over the side—"

"We are doomed!" said a feeble answering voice. "Let us die in peace!"

"There is still hope for us!" said the prince, untying the rope that bound him to the mast. "If we dive from the masthead we may overleap the sharks! All who have strength, arise and follow me!"

Weak and bruised as he was, the prince began to climb the swaying mast. When he reached the top, he clutched the masthead until the ship rolled so far over that he was carried halfway down to the heaving sea. Then he leaped outward and hurled himself into the water.

He struggled to the surface and struck out with all his strength, fleeing from the ship and the deadly ring of sharks. But where were his companions? He dared to look back and even called to them, but not a living soul was in sight. Each time the waves lifted him the prince would catch a glimpse of the foundering ship. She was sinking lower and lower until suddenly she slipped away under the sea and was gone. Prince Zanekka was alone.

He found a floating spar to rest on. His limbs had turned to lead and he could swim no farther. How long he clung to the spar he could not tell. He almost wished the storm clouds would return, for the sun rose in a brazen sky and scorched him cruelly. Once he fainted and lost his hold on the spar, recovering his senses just in time to save himself.

Now he understood the reason for his suffering. He was paying for disrespect and disobedience, the two sins he had committed against his mother. She loved him so dearly and more than once had risked her life for him. He had hurt her as no one else could. The tortures of heat and thirst, hunger and loneliness and even death by drowning—it was far better to endure these things in this life than undergo worse trials in lives to come. He was engulfed by a deep weariness and a strange feeling of peace.

Then it was that the good spirit, Megala Dewi, arrived to perform her special duty of saving people at sea—people who are destined for great things. Her strong gentle arms cradled the limp body of Prince Zanekka. The long day was waning, and in the low light of sunset she bore him swiftly over the sea toward the distant towers and temples of Thaton.

3

On the day of the shipwreck the town of Thaton was in a state of dire alarm. The people had heard nothing of the prince's mission; not even Zanekka's spies knew when he planned to set out from India to claim his birthright. All the talk in the streets and markets of the town was about the sudden death of the King of Thaton.

No one mourned for the cruel king or regretted the end of his reign of terror. Yet there was no gladness in Thaton. The future looked black, and the people's minds were filled with questions. Who was to succeed the king? Would a new ruler be worse than the old one?

Men sharpened their swords and knives and declared it was time for the people to rebel. They must put on the throne a man of their own choosing. Bandits and outlaws were known to be gathering in the city, waiting their chance to strike.

Behind the high walls of the royal palace the dead king's ministers were afraid of the rebellious spirit of the people. They sent an urgent invitation to the Principal Abbot of Thaton, an aged man renowned for his wisdom and learning. He arrived at the palace at sunset, and nine of the ministers met him in a small chamber next to the throne room.

The Abbot sat crosslegged on the carpet, calm and still. His eyes were cast down, and his dark brown robe contrasted with the rainbow silks of the ministers who knelt before him.

"Your Grace has been very good to come so quickly," the Chief Minister said.

The Abbot's shaven head bowed slightly in reply.

"We all agree that something must be done at once," the Minister went on, "but we cannot decide what course to take. The king is dead. His only son and heir was killed when hunting seven days ago. Your Grace must know that the people are restive, for the hand of the king was heavy upon them. At this very moment they may be plotting a rebellion. We fear they may choose as their leader some notorious *dacoit*—a murderer— and set him up as king. Therefore a new king must be found at once. But how shall we choose the right man?

"We beg Your Grace to use your deep wisdom and your power to see into the future, and to grant us the blessing of your advice."

A low murmur of approval came from the eight other ministers as their leader finished his speech.

The venerable Abbot looked into the worried eyes of the Chief Minister and answered in a strong, firm voice, with no trace of the weakness of old age.

"I knew you would wish to speak to me of the sudden death of the king," he said. "I have already studied the stars for guidance. There is nothing to fear, but old customs and traditions must be observed in the choice of the new king. Only if this is done will the people accept him. Now tell me—when the throne of Thaton is vacant, what is the traditional way of choosing a new king?"

The Chief Minister looked startled. "Surely Your Grace cannot mean the old custom of despatching an oxcart without a driver, to search for a new king?"

"That is indeed what I mean," the Abbot said. "Have faith. Invoke the good spirits of the palace and the city to guide the cart aright. Remember that the cart must be drawn by two young bulls, untrained to the yoke; and it must be loaded with the royal robes and crown and sword, together with food and drink for the new king. He will have need of all these things. . . ."

The last words, spoken in a low tone, puzzled the Chief Minister, but before he had time to ask a question, the Abbot spoke again. "Do you propose to follow my advice?"

The ministers answered in chorus: "Yes, Your Grace!" and their leader spoke for them all.

"We thank Your Grace for this excellent advice. We trust that the cart will find us the right man to be our king and that the people will accept him willingly. They know the ancient tradition, and we shall follow tradition in every way."

The Abbot was well pleased, and reminding them to send off the cart at daybreak next morning, he composed himself to receive their obeisance before he returned to his monastery.

 4

Before sunrise of the following day a huge silent crowd was gathered outside the palace of Thaton. The courtyard was filled with oxcarts and horsemen, but all eyes were on the cart that bore the regalia of the king. Strong men had to hold the two wild young bulls that were yoked to the cart. The beasts' angry bellowing almost drowned the chanted invocation to the spirits, who alone could guide the cart on its way.

As the first spear of sunlight shot into the courtyard, the chanting ceased. The jewelled crown and royal robes in the cart blazed as though they were on fire. The men let go of the bulls and sprang aside to clear the way, and the crowd let out a gasp of amazement.

Instead of throwing themselves into a desperate stampede, the bulls turned calmly toward the rising sun and moved forward, side by side, with the cart rumbling behind them. Through the east gate of the palace they went and then turned north along a lonely stretch of road. A line of carts followed, bearing the nobles and ministers of state, and in the midst of them walked the royal elephant with a golden howdah on his back, ready to carry the new king—if he could be found. Mounted retainers rode beside the carts, and the throng of people brought up the rear.

The faces of the ministers grew grim and the excited buzzing of the crowd died away when the people realized they were nearing the city's cemetery; but then the bulls turned westward and started across the grassy plain that bordered the sea. On and on they went to the sea's edge and halted with their forelegs in the water.

The Chief Minister, following close behind, gazed at the bulls in despair until he noticed a flat rock that jutted into the sea. Sprawling face downwards on the rock was the figure of a man.

The minister sprang from his cart and hurried over to the rock. His heart sank. The young man—for he was only a youth—lay very still, his lank wet hair streaming loose like seaweed. Could this be the new king, or had they come too late?

Soon the rock was surrounded by ministers and high dignitaries, and the people swarmed about them with a mighty shouting.

"A king! Our king is found! Behold our king!"

At the roar of voices the young man roused himself. He sat up to stare at the mass of people surrounding him, and in his eyes there was no fear—only the light of joy.

"My people!" he cried. "I am your king—your rightful king!"

Only the people nearest to him could hear his words, but as he sank down again, exhausted, a forest of hands reached out to touch him. Armed guards tried to hold back the crowd while servants gently lifted the young man and swathed his bruised limbs in silken wrappings. Food and drink appeared before him, and when he had eaten and gained strength, he was dressed in shining robes encrusted with gems. Finally a jewelled crown was placed on his head and he was carried to the royal elephant and enthroned in the golden howdah.

The elephant began to move toward the city. The ministers and noblemen formed a procession behind it, and all along the way the people danced and sang.

A new king had been found; a new and wonderful age had begun. This was enough to fill the saddest heart with thankfulness. But when the people learned that the cart had led them to the one man in all the world who was the rightful heir of Thaton, the whole land burst forth into wild rejoicing. Even after the feasts and dances were over and work began again, men, women and children still laughed and sang in the fields and the streets of the city. Merchants no longer cheated their customers, and the dreaded *dacoits* and outlaws came out of hiding and robbed and killed no more.

Even the Principal Abbot of Thaton was seen to smile at times, in spite of the solemn dignity of his office. He would gently mock the Chief Minister when they spoke together about the discovery of the king.

"I would that I had seen your face when you found him," the Abbot said. "You soon understood that I was right, and that he needed food and drink as well as robes. You did not wholeheartedly believe in the old tradition of the cart, did you?"

The Chief Minister shook his head. "How could Your Grace be so sure, in your wisdom, that our rightful king would be found by that means?"

"It was not so difficult," said the Abbot. "Remember that I had cast the horoscope of Prince Zanekka at his birth, as is the custom. On the death of his uncle, I consulted the horoscope again, and the stars told me that Prince Zanekka would be shipwrecked and then made king on his nineteenth birthday. So I knew that the unmanned cart would discover him on that day. His horoscope tells me also that he will be a good and noble king like his father."

And so it was. King Zanekka ruled wisely and well and was loved by his people. His mother was at his side to advise him in the early years of his reign, and with the help of his grandfather's state in South India King Zanekka made Thaton a famous centre of learning and enlightenment. The city became a shining jewel of the East, housing in its library the *Tripitaka,* the Three Baskets of Wisdom that contain the essence of Buddhist teaching.

These sacred books were to be coveted by one of the greatest kings of Burma, King Anawrahta of Pagan. How the *Tripitaka* and the written language came to Pagan is another story.

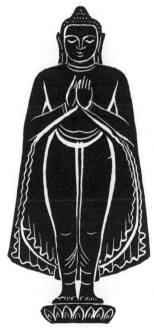

The Light of Truth

In the days when Thaton was the jewel of the East, re-nowned for its devotion to the Buddhist faith, the city of Pagan in the north was filled with bitterness and anguish.

Pagan was adorned with many temples, their tall pagodas rising above the Irrawaddy River; but instead of being places of enlightenment, joy and peace, the temples of Pagan were centres of tyranny and evil. The pure teachings of Buddha had been fouled by the dark practices of the *Ari* priests.

Long ago, when the first Ari priests had brought the Buddhist faith to Pagan from India, the people had welcomed them, not knowing that they were devil-worshippers and sorcerers, greedy for money and power. Laws were passed compelling the people to provide the priests with meat and strong drink and all they needed for a life of pleasure and dissipation. As the years passed and their burdens grew harder to bear, the people of Pagan longed to rebel, but the priests were too strong and too many for any man to resist them. They and their supporters could be counted in thousands. Even the king of Pagan, the fearless warrior Anawrahta, bowed to their will.

It was in the reign of Anawrahta that a man from Thaton arrived in the troubled city. He was a tall, spare man dressed in a plain brown robe. His head was shaven, smooth as old ivory. The brow was high and the nose thin and straight. His lips showed gentleness and humour, but on this day his mouth was set in a firm line and his eyes burned with inner fire.

Stepping ashore from the dugout canoe that had carried him up the river, the stranger strode through the city gate, unnoticed by the crowds of people passing in and out. He walked swiftly through the streets, looking neither right nor left, until he came to the gateway of the royal palace. When the guards questioned him, he had only to mention his name, Shin Arahan, and he was welcomed inside with reverence. He was a stranger in Pagan, but the fame of his deep learning had marched

before him, and King Anawrahta was pleased to grant him an audience without delay.

They met in the throne room, but the king, out of respect for his visitor, came down from his throne. The two men sat on a carpet, face to face, the dark-robed priest and the warrior king.

"Our city is honoured by your presence here," said Anawrahta. "We have heard of your greatness among the priests of Thaton, and of the pure lives of the monks in your monasteries. We hear they eat but one meal a day and take no food after midday, and that they never touch meat or strong drink. It is also said that they sleep little and spend many hours in preaching, meditation and prayer. Can this indeed be true? Our priests are fat, pot-bellied beings; they feast and drink and satisfy their lusts. Tell me, how does the teaching of Buddha produce such different results?"

Shin Arahan had listened with bent head, but now his burning eyes stared straight at the king. "Sire," he exclaimed, "your Ari priests are false! They are not Buddhists!"

"But they brought the Buddhist faith to Pagan," said the king, "long years ago, from India—"

"Their faith is false and evil! They do not practice or preach the teachings of Buddha. From my youth I have heard of their black deeds and of the devil-worship that terrorizes your people, and for years I have studied and prepared myself to come to Pagan and cast out the evil-doers! I am here to bring you the Master's teaching in all its purity, to sweep away evil and to flood your darkness with light!"

The words were like tongues of flame, and now it was the king who bowed his head. He knew the power of the Ari priests, the strength of their stranglehold upon the land. He was ashamed of his surrender to their tyranny, but in his heart he feared them.

He hid his shame by smiling and spoke half in jest. "Would you turn us all into vegetarian ascetics?"

"No, Sire," said Shin Arahan. "There are more important matters than refraining from eating meat. The followers of Buddha do good works, help others and thus gain merit for themselves in their future lives. They practice self-control and self-discipline and they have compassion for all living things."

The priest leaned forward and spread out his thin hands. "Think, Sire, how your country will be changed when the people follow the path of Buddha! There will be peace and contentment, and some men will even break out of the cycle of birth and suffering and death and attain true enlightenment."

A mysterious inner peace was reflected in the face of the monk, and the king spoke quietly in reply. "You have said enough to make me want to know more. May I invite you to live at the palace and instruct me in this teaching?"

"Most certainly, Sire," said Shin Arahan. "Part of my life's work will be done when Your Majesty has learned the pure doctrine that the Master left to the world."

So the monk of Thaton came daily to teach the king, and Anawrahta was amazed as he listened. Each day found him more determined to destroy the Ari temples and break the dread power of the priests. But first the pure teachings had to be passed on to all the people. The blessings of the Way had to be revealed to everyone, great and small.

"How can this be done?" he demanded of Shin Arahan. "How can the people be taught?"

"I must start a school," said the priest, "to train young men who can go forth and teach others throughout the land. But it will not be easy, for in Pagan you have no written language. We cannot write down the scriptures on palm-leaf pages and make books that men may study and learn by heart. Above all, we need the *Tripitaka*—the Three Baskets of Wisdom—the great book that contains the heart of the Master's teaching and has been for me a lifelong study."

To Anawrahta, a man of action and a warrior, this talk of books was strange, but now he would have given half his kingdom to hold the *Tripitaka* in his grasp. Instinctively his hand moved to his sword. "How can we get this book?" he demanded.

"King Manuha of Thaton has thirty copies of the *Tripitaka*," said Shin Arahan. "He might be persuaded to lend you one. Then we could translate the text into the language of Pagan and write it down in the script they use in Thaton. Thereby you would not only have the scriptures but also a means of writing more books to spread the light of learning in your land!"

"This shall be done!" said Anawrahta. "I will send a mission to Thaton at once with costly gifts. King Manuha will be unable to refuse our request and the book will be ours!"

Two weeks later a splendid procession wound its way to the city gates of Thaton. At its head rode a prince of Pagan, mounted on a royal elephant. Behind him came twenty noblemen on horseback with a host of attendants and bearers of golden umbrellas. Heralds had been sent ahead to announce the arrival of the prince, and he expected to find the gates wide open to receive him. Instead, they were firmly closed.

The prince was taken aback, and some of the proud young nobles, burning with rage at the insult, were ready to return home at once. But the counsel of older men prevailed.

"King Manuha is only doing this to try us," they said. "He and his people take us for barbarians. Have patience and we can show them this is not so."

Presently a haughty emissary emerged from the gate, resplendent in silk of peacock blue, and addressed the party in the language of Pagan. One of the older noblemen replied politely in the Mon speech of Thaton, and the emissary was so startled and impressed that he promptly obtained permission for the party to enter.

People came running from houses and bazaars to watch the procession pass along the principal street of the city to the royal palace. The palace gates were opened to the prince from Pagan, but when he and his nobles were granted an audience with the king, they were received with scant courtesy.

King Manuha, seated crosslegged on his golden throne, accepted the gifts from Pagan without a word and hardly glanced at the rolls of shining silk, the bright diadems and the magnificent jewelled sword. He listened coldly to the request for a copy of the *Tripitaka* and replied in a tone of scorn.

"Perhaps King Anawrahta, not being a man of learning, does not know that Thaton is justly famed for the glory of its scholarship. Its fame is based on the study of the *Tripitaka* and the commentaries that have been written by the wisest scholars. These books are beyond price. Yet the king of a country overrun by devil-worshippers, a country that does not even possess a written language, has the temerity to ask for these precious scriptures. King Anawrahta does not know what he asks. My answer to him is an emphatic 'No.'

"The audience is ended."

When the mission returned empty-handed to Pagan, the wrath of King Anawrahta was terrible. Even Shin Arahan failed to calm him or to persuade him to have patience. Pagan must have the scriptures, the king said, and if two hundred holy monks, instead of one, had tried to dissuade him, they could not have changed his resolution. The *Tripitaka* must be seized by force of arms.

 3

King Anawrahta threw himself into preparations for a military campaign. This was a task he understood, and one in which Shin Arahan could not help him. The monk was grieved by the turn of events and quietly retired to the house the king had built for him. There he began training young men in the true teachings of Buddha. Daily their voices could be heard in chorus, reciting the scriptures, while in the Ari temples the fat priests still feasted and wove their dark spells.

Fighting men poured into the city to join the king's army; hammers clanged night and day in the workshops of smiths and sword makers, and at last a great column of foot soldiers, horsemen and huge war elephants was ready to set out. With a burst of cheering and a clamour of gongs and drums the king led them forth to Thaton.

The journey southward was long and hard and many days passed before news of the army came back to

Pagan. The king had laid siege to Thaton, for the city could not be taken by storm. Its high walls were defended by crossbowmen who shot with deadly aim if the attackers came within range. When the men of Pagan charged the city gates, some were crushed by boulders hurled down from above and others burned alive by buckets of boiling pitch.

The siege dragged on. Nearly three months passed, and King Anawrahta was no nearer to his goal. The citizens of Thaton showed no sign of hardship, and each time the king launched an attack he lost more men. Yet Anawrahta refused to give up.

If the city could not be taken by force, other means must be used. Five men might achieve what five thousand had failed to do, and in the king's household there were five men whom he trusted above all others. He summoned them to the royal tent and impatiently awaited their coming.

The leader of the five was Kyanzitha, who was said to be the king's own son. The young man's mother had been one of Anawrahta's lesser queens, a princess from Assam. The king had sent her away to a village up the Chindwin River where Kyanzitha was born. In looks the boy resembled neither his mother nor the king, but like Anawrahta he had grown up to be a courageous fighter, and he loved the king as though they were of one blood.

The exploits of Kyanzitha's four friends had become a legend. Nyaung Uphi was a famous swimmer; Nga Lon Te Pe had been a ploughman and possessed the strength of an elephant; and Ngo Htwe Yu was a fearless climber who had learned his skill as a boy by climbing tall toddy-palms. Finally there was Kyanzitha's boon companion, Byatta, an Indian whose story was the strangest of all.

He and his twin brother, Byatwi, had been shipwrecked when they were children and cast ashore on the coast near Thaton. They had been rescued by a monk of that city and brought up to be servants in his monastery.

The monk was revered by King Manuha of Thaton, and one day he was called to the palace. He was busy roasting some meat that had mysterious supernatural properties, and he left the twins with orders to turn the spit but not to touch the roast. The smell was so tempting that they finally tasted the meat and soon had eaten every scrap. Suddenly they found themselves filled with tremendous strength. They promptly turned the monastery upside down, and when the venerable monk returned he was aghast. He made them set the monastery to rights and then marched them off to King Manuha.

Young as they were, the twins each had the strength of ten men. They could toss an ox over their shoulders or wrestle a rogue elephant to a standstill, and they performed such prodigious feats of arms that the king himself began to fear them.

He issued secret orders for the twins to be captured and put to death. Assassins went to Byatwi's house at night and killed him while he slept. They chopped his body into four pieces which were buried at the four corners of the city, and they laid a trail of his blood around the city walls. Thus the spirit of Byatwi was chained forever to the walls of Thaton, to defend the city with the mighty strength that he had had in life.

Byatta, who could run with the speed of lightning, had fled to Pagan and entered the service of King Anawrahta as a messenger. He longed to avenge the murder of his brother, and his heart cried out for battle as he and his four companions obeyed the royal summons and hurried to Anawrahta's tent.

They knelt before the king and he addressed them at once. "The siege of Thaton must be brought to an end. Boredom and idleness have sapped the fighting spirit of our men. Food is running short and in a month the rainy season will be upon us, when we can no longer stay in the field. We must act now!

"You five must find a way to enter the city in secret, and in secret you must strike from within! The fate of all of us—the fate of Pagan itself—depends on you."

4

The band of five reached the shadow of the city wall at the dead of night. Thaton lay silent and asleep; no man had seen them. While four of the band crouched in the blackness, the toddy-palm climber began to scale the wall. He had pulled himself up and over the edge when the others heard a muffled cry and his body hurtled down and hit the ground with a thump. They ran to him and knelt at his side.

He lay winded and gasping but unharmed. He had been saved from injury by the amulet he wore around his neck and the blue tattoo-patterns on his limbs— strong magic against the effects of blows and falls.

"What happened?" whispered Kyanzitha, and the four men waited, holding their breath, until Nga Htwe Yu could speak.

"I had climbed on the top of the wall," he whispered at last, "and I stood up, and then—then a huge black

giant of a man swung a mighty club at my head. I
ducked, but my shoulder took the blow and—I fell!"

"How could he see you?" Kyanzitha demanded. "Was
he waiting for you?"

"No, no one was on the wall," gasped Nga Htwe Yu.
"I looked long and hard before climbing on top. I swear
there was no one! Then suddenly, in the blink of an eye,
he appeared!"

"My brother!" groaned Byatta. "It was the spirit of
my murdered brother!"

For a moment the others stared at him in horror.
Then Kyanzitha spoke. "Byatta, if this is true indeed
and it is your brother, could you—speak to him?"

"*Speak* to him?" Byatta's naked sword gleamed in the
darkness. "What is the use of that? What must I say?"

"Ask your brother how we can enter the city," said
Kyanzitha. "He must know a way. Tell him that once
we have taken Thaton his remains will be dug up from
the corners of the city wall. He will be given a funeral
and monks will recite *Mantras* to snap asunder the
magic bonds that hold him to the wall. Thus we shall
set him free."

A few moments later Nga Htwe Yu was climbing the
wall again with a long rope in his teeth. He fastened the
rope firmly to a projecting beam near the top, and
when he had slid to the ground Byatta began to climb
the rope stealthily, hand over hand. Standing on the
beam, he could reach the top of the wall with his fingers. He had heaved himself over the edge when the

huge black figure took shape before him, a massive club in its hand ready to strike.

"O my brother!" said Byatta. "What has their black magic done to you? Do you not know me? I am Byatta —strike me not! I have not yet crossed the trail of your blood that circles the city, so you cannot and you shall not strike me!"

The club was lowered, and a hollow voice spoke from the tall black figure. "O brother, I am a prisoner here, in servitude forever, compelled to strike whoever crosses the line of blood. Keep back, brother, for you know my strength!"

Byatta balanced on the outer edge of the wall. "Listen, O spirit of Byatwi!" he said. "My four friends and I must enter the city. Thaton must be taken by King Anawrahta, our leader, for the sake of his people, the people of Pagan, who seek to know the Way of Buddha —and for your sake too, my brother! Help us and we shall set you free! Is there no unprotected place where we may enter?"

"There is one place only," answered the hollow voice. "At the southwest corner of the city a small banyan tree leans over the wall. At that place no blood was spilt, for none was left to spill. There is a space of one cubit's breadth on which your feet may tread. I have no power to defend that spot. Go there, brother, and make haste. But return, Byatta! Do not forget! I await my release!"

And so the five gained entry to the city.

Byatta knew Thaton like the palm of his hand, and in

serving King Manuha he had learned to know the houses of the noblemen and ministers of state and the habits of their owners. That night, while all Thaton lay sleeping, three ministers and three army commanders were mysteriously slain.

For five successive nights the terror went on. Each morning brought news of death in yet another noble household. Wild alarm swept through the ranks of the high and mighty, and defenses were doubled at the palace of King Manuha.

One of the latest victims was a prince of the royal house, and beside his body a message was found, written in bold Mon characters: "O Manuha, surrender with good grace, and mercy will be shown to you. Refuse, and you and your house will be destroyed. Death will be sure and imminent."

On the sixth morning of the secret scourge the people found a written proclamation nailed up in the main marketplace, at the law court and at the entrance to the principal pagoda.

"We have not come to destroy you," the message read. "We of Pagan requested a loan of the scriptures from your arrogant king who added insults to his refusal. We still ask for the scriptures. We shall spare the lives of the king and his family, and of all who lay down their arms.

"Surrender now! Surrender before we break down the gates, scale the walls and put everyone to the sword. We will give you three days' grace, but the sooner you surrender the sooner you shall have freedom, ease and comfort once again.

"I, Anawrahta of Pagan, proclaim this."

Manuha of Thaton surrendered.

The gates of the city were opened to the army of Pagan, and the king was led out with a chain of gold around his neck, proof that Anawrahta could be merciful and gracious to a foe.

Even in the hour of triumph the murdered Byatwi was not forgotten. As soon as the troops had entered the city, Byatwi's remains were dug up and brought together for burial. A hundred monks of Thaton chanted *Mantras*, the sacred verses that would release his tortured spirit from its slavery, and the written order for the release was sealed by King Anawrahta, as conqueror and ruler of Thaton.

Then the victorious king led his men through the streets to the Royal Monastery to find the *Tripitaka*. The precious book that King Manuha had refused him was his at last. He held in his hands the frail palm-leaf pages that would bring the light of faith to his people. But now Anawrahta had won more than a book. The whole city lay at his mercy, and all the riches of Thaton were his to command.

The royal palace, the temples and the monasteries must be stripped of their treasures. The monks of Thaton were set to work packing the volumes of sacred scriptures, the holy relics and the most beautiful of the images. Not only the works of art but the artists and

craftsmen who had made them were to be carried away
to Pagan, and five hundred monks were to join Shin
Arahan in spreading the true faith among Anawrahta's
people.

When at last the king's army was ready for the home-
ward march, they left Thaton a silent, haunted place,
an empty shell from which the life had fled.

 5

The news of King Anawrahta's victory was carried
swiftly to Pagan, and on the day of the army's return
the people streamed out of the city to welcome the con-
querors.

A ringing cheer rose from the crowd when the van-
guard of the triumphal procession came marching up
the road to the rhythm of gongs and drums. Then the
king himself appeared, mounted on an elephant with

trappings of red and gold, and beside him were the five companions who had served him so well. Men, women and children pressed forward to greet the king, tossed flowers in his path and called down blessings on the five heroes.

Following Anawrahta were the captive King Manuha and his queen and some of the highest nobles of Thaton. Then came thirty-two white elephants loaded with treasures and behind them an endless string of crafts-men, artists and monks from the conquered city, strag-gling wearily on horseback and on foot. Soldiers and wagons and pack horses brought up the rear, and the people closed in behind them to march into Pagan for celebrations that would last till dawn.

Yet there were many in the city for whom this was a black day. The Ari priests looked out from the darkness of their temples, and curses were in their hearts and on their lips. Above all, as the procession passed them by, they stared with hatred at the ranks of shaven-headed monks from Thaton. They saw these lean quiet men as a threat to their power, a threat that could no longer be denied.

The Ari priests had laughed at the preaching of Shin Arahan, for how could they be shaken by the effort of a single man? Their iron control over the people was stronger than ever; they had supporters in high places, and as for the king—he would not dare attack them! But what now? Would the king turn from them and listen only to the teachings of these men of Thaton?

Within a few days the Ari priests had the king's answer. A royal decree proclaimed that the Ari temples
were temples of wickedness and must be destroyed.

The priests heard the news, unbelieving. Many of
them were drowsing in drunken sleep when the king's
men rushed into the temples. Soldiers drove out the
priests with swords and spears and flung flaming torches
into the sanctuaries. Fire roared through the roofs of
the temples, pagodas came crashing down, images
melted like wax and the whole city was veiled in foul
black smoke.

The priests were herded into the streets, shouting and
protesting, struggling and weeping. In vain they threatened their tormentors with curses and black magic and
called upon the people to stand by them. The head
priests were gathered together and banished, driven at
sword's point over the border of the kingdom. The
lesser men were seized for the king's service and condemned to be cleaners of the royal stables, keepers of
elephants and sweepers of the courtyards of the palace.

Nobles and men of power, who had supported the Ari
priests, were banished with them, and the people of
Pagan, so long oppressed, were set free at last. It seemed
as though all fear and evil were consumed in the pillars
of smoke from the burning temples. Then the rains
came to wash the city clean, and in the freshness of the
air the calm voices of the monks of Thaton could be
heard chanting the scriptures.

The people flocked to listen to the teachers of the new

faith. They could hardly believe that the Way of Buddha led not to cruel sacrifices and dark magic but to peace and gentleness and compassion. While Shin Arahan and the monks taught the people, they also worked night and day to write down the scriptures in the language of Pagan. Within a year the city had a written language of its own that could be used in books and even inscribed on slabs of stone that men might read in centuries to come.

With the help of the artists and craftsmen of Thaton, new and beautiful temples were built at King Anawrahta's command. Even the captive King Manuha, who had been given a palace to live in with his family, was allowed to supervise the making of a pagoda that bore his name. A massive brick building, the *Tripitaka-taik,* was set up to house the sacred scriptures, and it can still be seen today among the ruins of ancient Pagan.

The reign of King Anawrahta was the beginning of a golden age for the city on the Irrawaddy River. Long after his life was done, the kings of Pagan continued to build temples. A forest of shining pinnacles reached to the skies, reminding all men to follow in the path of Buddha.

Some of the greatest temples stand in glory to this day among the crumbling ruins of hundreds of smaller shrines. Pagan, the city of five thousand temples, still bears witness to the faith of one man, Shin Arahan, who came from Thaton so long ago to conquer evil and to lead the people into truth and light.

The Gift

It was night and the clear-shining face of the moon looked down over the treetops of the great forest. Far below there was a clearing among the trees, and in the bright moonlight three friends had come together there —the rabbit, the otter, and the crow.

The rabbit looked up at the moon and said: "Alas, it will be full moon tomorrow, when we must all go to the temple with our offerings, and I have nothing to give!"

"Perhaps I can help you," said the otter.

"Hush!" said the crow. "Beware! There's a man coming. Don't look yet!"

Then his voice changed. "Why, it's an old, old man, and he seems to be ill."

The otter and the rabbit turned around to look, and sure enough they saw a feeble old man leaning on a bamboo staff. He came tottering towards them and collapsed on the ground to rest.

"I am so tired and hungry," he moaned. "I shall surely die in this wild forest."

"Be of good cheer, Sir," said the crow, hopping up beside him. "I have some cake that I was keeping as an offering for tomorrow. You shall have it." And away he flew.

"And I," said the otter, "will bring you the fish I was keeping for tomorrow." And off he went to the nearby stream.

But the rabbit had nothing to give. And he well knew that the poor old man needed far more than a small fish and a piece of cake to keep him alive. What he really should have was some fresh meat.

Suddenly the rabbit leaped into the air in great joy.

"Venerable Sir," he said to the old man. "I have something for you, something to give you strength and life. But my gift will need cooking. Can you make a fire?"

"Of course I can make a fire," said the old man, "and it will warm me within and without!"

He bustled about with surprising energy, collecting leaves and twigs, sticks and faggots. In no time at all a fire was roaring in the middle of the clearing, and the old man sat down happily to warm himself.

The crow and the otter were surprised to see the fire when they returned with their gifts. Then their surprise turned to amazement and horror, for there, before their eyes, their friend the rabbit shook himself from

head to toe, threw back his head and leaped straight into the heart of the flames.

But instead of writhing in pain, with his fur and flesh on fire, the rabbit was enthroned upon a cool green lotus leaf, quite unharmed. The flames and smoke licked about him, but not a hair of his body was singed. More amazing and bewildering still, the old man had vanished, as though he had never been.

Then a deep hush filled the forest clearing, and out of the silence came a gentle voice, the voice of the overlord of the spirits, the great good spirit and destroyer of all evil.

"Thank you, thank you for your generous gifts, my friends," the spirit said. "Not only was the rabbit ready to die that I might live, but at the very moment of plunging into the fire he remembered to shake off the fleas from his body, to save them from death in the flames. So that all creatures everywhere may remember this night's noble deed the face of the moon shall forever bear a sign."

As the voice ceased, a cloud hid the face of the moon. When the cloud drifted away, the friends gazed up at the moon in wonder. Its clear and unblemished face was marked by a strange shadow.

And so it has remained ever since. If at the next full moon you look very carefully, just as the rabbit, the otter and the crow did so long ago, you too will see the shadow on the moon's face, and its shape will be the shape of the rabbit.

The City of the Dagger

1

Princess Mimosa

Long, long ago a great warrior ruled over China. Fighting was his sport and joy, and he was never happier than when he could test his strength on the battlefield.

Only one thing made him sad. As the years went by and he conquered more and more land for his kingdom, he longed to have a son. He needed a boy who would not only learn the arts of war but shoulder the burden

of governing the mighty empire. But the Emperor of China had no son; he had seven daughters.

Although a family of girls was a calamity for a ruler and a man of war, the Emperor refused to be defeated by his misfortune. He resolved to bring up his daughters as sons. He hired the finest instructors to train them in warfare and in sport. The seven princesses learned to run and swim and ride, to shoot with bow and arrow and to wield a sword with strength and skill. While their bodies grew tough and tireless, their minds were trained in scholarship, law and ancient learning, to prepare them for the duties of government. At last the Emperor considered them ready for the life he had planned.

It was the eighteenth birthday of the youngest of the seven, the beautiful Princess Mimosa. The streets of the capital city were hung with red banners, rows of fluttering flags and paper lamps, and crowds of people waited outside the palace gates to see the royal procession.

The vast throne room of the palace was thronged with dignitaries from every corner of the empire, gathered there for the birthday of the princess. All stood at attention as the hall reverberated to the thunder of a giant gong and the royal procession moved to the dais. The Emperor took his seat on a huge red and gold throne. The seven princesses, dressed in shining silver armour and girt with swords, took their places on smaller thrones in front of him.

Again the gong sounded, and then the Emperor spoke.

"Officials and representatives of my people, I bid you welcome. We are here to bring in a new order. Today I am appointing each of my seven daughters to be governor of a province. They are well trained and ready, and with soldiers and statesmen to help them, they will bring good government to the farthest corners of the empire."

One by one, he summoned the seven princesses, beginning with the eldest, and each received from him the great seal of her province and a jade ring carved with the royal insignia. Last of all, the Emperor called the Princess Mimosa, his favourite daughter. "And to you," he said, "I give the Province of Yunan. May you govern it well!"

Yunan was the rockiest, most harsh and wild of the provinces, bordering on the mountains of Tibet! The heart of the youngest princess beat violently and she longed to protest, but she was too well-schooled to show her feelings. She humbly accepted the seal and ring, then turned to bow to the gathering and to follow her sisters in a glittering procession through the city streets.

Within a week of the birthday celebrations the seven princesses, with their retinues of soldiers, servants and advisers, were on the way to take up their new duties. The Princess Mimosa found her province as grim and inhospitable as she had known it would be—a very different world from her father's brilliant court.

Yet Princess Mimosa, like the Emperor himself, refused to bow down under misfortune. Her people might be rough and wild and hard to govern, but their rugged country was the finest hunting ground she had ever seen. Whenever she was weary of state affairs, she could mount her horse and chase the leaping deer over the hills.

Within two years she had hunted everywhere in her domain. The best hunting ground of all lay on the frontier with Tibet. This, she knew, was forbidden territory. Too many battles had been fought there between the Tibetans and the Chinese, and the Emperor had warned the princess to keep clear of the Tibetans and to leave them strictly alone in their mountain strongholds.

But when Princess Mimosa was hunting, she cared not a fig for her father's advice. Her chief huntsman warned her to turn back from the forbidden borderland, but she only laughed at him and accused him of ruining her sport.

That day the princess was hot on the trail of a magnificent golden stag. Leaving her party far behind, she galloped on and on along the narrow mountain trails with the great stag bounding ahead. At last she tossed aside her horse's reins and drew back her bow for the kill. Just as she loosed the arrow, the horse stumbled heavily among the rocks. The princess was flung to the ground and lay on the stony path as though she were dead.

When she came to herself and opened her eyes, she was looking up into the face of a young man. "You must be Princess Mimosa," he said. "Since you have come to

hunt here, I have followed you and watched you from afar, hoping with all my heart that we might meet."

The princess, bruised and battered as she was, sat up and tried to speak with royal dignity. "Who are you?" she demanded. "What do you mean by spying on me?"

"I cannot tell you now," said the young man, "but meet me tomorrow at midday in the cave near your hunting lodge—the hidden cave under the walnut tree. Then I will make myself known."

He sprang to his feet and with four long strides he had vanished among the rocks. The princess sat gazing after him until her hunting party came clattering down the trail to find her.

The next day she met the young man in the cave by the walnut tree, and they met every day after that, as long as she stayed to hunt in the borderland. But it is hard for a princess to do anything secretly. The sharp eyes of her servants followed her. Her counsellors received whispered messages and tugged their beards in alarm. Messengers were sent galloping through the mountains and over the dusty plains to the capital city, and the Emperor received the terrible news that Princess Mimosa was in love with the Crown Prince of Tibet.

The Emperor's rage was like an exploding volcano. With an armed retinue he rode by forced marches to the capital of Yunan. The cruel pace of the journey brought on his gout and made his fury more violent than ever. When he reached the palace of the princess, he swept aside her polite greeting and confronted her, with the dust of the journey still thick upon his armour.

"This is high treason!" he roared in a voice of thunder. "Did I not warn you to have nothing to do with the Tibetans? And now, what do I find? My daughter, the Governor of Yunan, preparing to marry the Crown Prince of Tibet and to give him, as her marriage dowry, the Province of Yunan, the land I entrusted to her care! To think that I have trained you and taught you all you know, only to see you betray me! You have earned a traitor's death!"

Princess Mimosa stood before him, straight and stiff as a soldier on parade. "But I am innocent, father," she said. "My first meeting with the prince came by accident, and never have we spoken a word concerning our two countries. We love each other, but is that a crime? Is it an offense to love?"

"Then what is this I hear about an army gathering in Tibet to seize your province and carry you off to marry the Crown Prince?"

"It is all a terrible lie, father," said the princess. "I know of no such plan."

The Emperor swung around and strode furiously up and down the room. Had she been a son, he might have killed her for her treason; but she was his favourite daughter, too young perhaps to know what she was doing.

Again he faced her, and she met his gaze without flinching. "Daughter," he said, "this is the last time I shall speak to you. You cannot be left here as governor. Nor can you live elsewhere in China, to be a living proof of the failure of my plan to treat my daughters as sons. By rights, you should die for your treason. Instead, you shall be banished. May the spirits of our ancestors protect and guide you!"

The Emperor's orders were carried out that same night. Under cover of darkness Princess Mimosa was taken away from the capital of Yunan, guarded by a company of horsemen. They rode westward for many days until they came to a swift river near the frontier of the empire. Woodsmen in the party cut down trees along the shore and lashed them together to make a raft. Two days later, the men heaved the raft into the water and loaded it with sacks, jars and carved chests, containing food and supplies for a long journey. Then they gently helped the princess to climb aboard and pushed her out into the stream.

The current seized the raft and whirled it away, and the men watched in silence. As long as they could see her the princess sat stiff and erect, but when the raft had rounded a bend in the river and the men were hidden from sight, her loneliness and sorrow were too much for her to bear. She bowed down among the bags and bundles and wept as though her heart would break.

 2

The Two Princes

For a long time Princess Mimosa crouched among her belongings on the raft, worn out with weeping, while the current swept her on downstream, deeper into the unknown. Then she remembered her training and felt ashamed of her weakness. Calling upon the spirits of her ancestors to help her, she grasped the large steering oar, lashed amidships, and guided the raft on its way.

When the evening sun cast long shadows, she steered her craft to a big tree in a backwater and tied up for the night. By first light the raft was on the move again, and for many days the princess journeyed on downstream, travelling where the river led her.

At last the raft slid into the upper reaches of the Irrawaddy, the great river that flows down through Burma. Princess Mimosa, weary to the bone, noticed only that the water was deep and swift-flowing, the air calm and filled with sweet scents from the forest along the shore. As the sun dipped behind the trees she fell into an exhausted sleep. She did not see the harsh line of cliffs on the left bank. While she slept the current carried her nearer and nearer to that black rocky shore until a swirl of water pushed the raft through the hidden entrance of a huge cave.

The princess woke with a start as the raft ran aground on a shelving beach. Someone lifted her up and she thought she was dreaming. Then a shaft of moonlight shot through a break in the rocky roof and the princess gasped in amazement and joy.

"O my prince!" she cried. "You have found me at last!"

The young man who held her in his arms had the face and form of the Crown Prince of Tibet, appearing by some miracle when she needed him most. She was too weak and weary that night for him to talk to her. Later he confessed that he was not the prince but a good spirit, condemned to take the shape of a tiger by day and a human shape only at night. Being a spirit and not a mortal man, he had been able to look into the past of the princess and to take the form of the Tibetan prince she loved.

The great Golden Cave by the riverside was his home, and there he cared for the princess and comforted her after her long lonely journey. She came to love him, even though she knew he was not her prince, and two sons were born to them.

All through their childhood the boys were aware of some mystery about their birth and their parents, which their mother thought they were too young to understand. When they were seventeen and eighteen years old, they stood before her and insisted on knowing the truth. Then she told them her whole strange story, beginning with her childhood at the court of the Emperor of China, the warrior with seven daughters and no son.

The boys listened with growing excitement, hardly able to keep silent to the end. "So you, our mother, are Princess Mimosa!" exclaimed the younger son.

"And our grandfather," said the elder one, "is the Emperor of China! Let us go to him, Mother! He will want to hear news of you and to see us, your sons."

"Oh, I was afraid of this," said the princess. "Must I lose both of you? Please stay with me!"

"But we *must* go, Mother," they said. "Your father, the Emperor, would wish it."

The princess bowed her head. "Go with my blessing then, my sons," she said. "By day a tiger shall watch over you on your journey, and by night, a mighty warrior. Take this jade ring. Never part with it until you place it in your grandfather's hand. He will recognize the carving and the royal insignia, and he will know you to be his grandsons indeed. But when you have seen him, come back to me, my sons!"

The two boys set out on their journey armed with bows and arrows, spears and swords. As the princess had promised, a great tiger padded along the path before them all day, and at night their sleep was guarded by a warrior, tall as a giant and silent as a statue.

The brothers travelled on and on, through forests, over mountains and rolling plains, sometimes through towns and villages and often in wilderness, far from the homes of men. They were tired and hungry, battered by rain or blinded by storms of dust. When they came at last to the capital city of the Emperor of China, their bodies were gaunt and their clothes were faded rags.

It was evening and their friendly escort, the tiger, had vanished, his duty done. To the crowds of people in the city streets the young princes were just a pair of beggars. Mockery and laughter greeted them when they stopped at the gate of the Imperial Palace and asked to be let in.

"What is your business?" called the gatekeeper through a little window in the huge gate.

"We would see the Emperor," said the older brother.

"And what business have you with the Emperor?"

"That is not for you to know," said the younger brother. "We come from a faraway land with news for the Emperor's ear alone."

"Behold this ring!" said the older brother. "We must place it in the Emperor's hand."

"Give it to me," sneered the gatekeeper. "*I'll* give it to the Emperor."

As he spoke there was a clatter of hoofs from within, followed by a sharp word of command, and the little window shut with a bang. Then the great gate slowly opened wide, and a company of horsemen, gay in gleaming silks, came trotting out. The haughty mandarin who rode in the midst of them looked down in scorn at the two brothers. "And who are these," he said, "who dare to linger at the Emperor's gate?"

"O Excellency," answered the gatekeeper, "they have a jade ring to give to the Emperor."

The mandarin's eyebrows shot up in surprise. "Who are you?" he demanded.

"We are grandsons of the Emperor," said the two brothers.

"Grandsons of the Emperor? I know of no such thing," said the mandarin. "Who is your mother?"

"Princess Mimosa of Yunan," came the proud reply.

"But the princess was banished twenty years ago!"

The long fingers of the mandarin trembled on the reins of his horse. Twenty years ago he had led the party who were the last men in China to see the princess alive. It had torn his heart to watch her swept away down the river on her raft.

He hid his feelings under a show of anger. "How do I know you are not lying? Show me the ring!"

He stared at the carvings and the royal insignia, then swung his horse around and rode back through the gate, commanding the boys to follow him. The gatekeeper stood aside to let them pass and wished devoutly he had been more civil to the grandsons of the Emperor.

Across the broad courtyards of the palace and through the tall portal of the throne room the brothers followed the mandarin, and at last they stood before the Emperor. He towered above them, enthroned on the high dais, a huge square man, strong as an elephant and with the proud fierce eyes of a tiger. The two brothers gazed up at him fearlessly while the mandarin explained who they were and presented the jade ring.

One glance at the ring and the Emperor welcomed the boys with open arms. Servants were sent scurrying hither and thither to prepare food and baths and beds for them after their long journey, and to bring them garments of the softest silk. Nothing was too good for the grandsons of the Emperor, the sons of his favourite daughter! The Emperor's pain and sorrow at his daughter's treason and banishment were forgotten in the joy of knowing she still lived and the even greater joy of welcoming her sons.

Feasting and making merry began in the palace that very day, and all the town was on holiday while the princes were there. Mounted on magnificent horses, they rode out to visit their six aunts, the capable governors of six provinces. Everywhere the people rejoiced to see them and to hear that Princess Mimosa was alive and well. As for the Emperor, he was as proud of the boys as if they had been sons of his own. He was overjoyed with their skill in riding, shooting and swordplay. It warmed his heart to know that their mother had trained them in body and mind to be worthy grandsons of her warrior-father.

The Emperor longed to keep them at his side, and the boys would have been happy to stay, but they could not forget their mother, waiting for them far away. They begged leave to go home.

"I know, my grandsons," said the Emperor sadly, "that I must let you return to your mother and to the country of your future. In that land—not here in China —you can make the fullest use of your talents. But I shall not send you away empty-handed. Each of you shall have a thousand horsemen and five hundred war-elephants, a thousand archers and a train of mules and baggage horses. These forces shall be commanded, under your leadership, by the best officers from my army, and you shall each have three wise counsellors to advise you in peace and war. All these shall await you tomorrow, a day's march from the city.

"But the greatest gifts I can give you are small enough to carry in your hands. These have been wrought by master magicians, weaving spells and incantations to secure for you fair fortune in the years to come."

The Emperor beckoned to the older brother and handed him an ordinary brass gong and a short, felt-topped cane for beating it.

"Once you have left China," he said, "you must beat this gong each night at the place where you intend to camp. It will make no sound until you have reached the centre of the territory where your kingdom is to be. Having found that central spot, you may push the boundaries of your realm as far outward as you desire."

Then he turned to the younger brother and held out to him a dagger with a wide double-edged blade. "Wherever you make camp, throw this dagger to the ground. When the blade pierces the earth and stands upright, you will have reached your future kingdom."

As the younger brother grasped the dagger, the silver handle pressed into his palm and the keen edges of the steel winked and glinted in the sun.

The two brothers bowed before the Emperor and thanked him again and again for his generosity. A small band of horsemen waited for them in the courtyard of the palace. They mounted their horses, and the gate-keeper sprang to open the gate.

From a high window of the palace the Emperor watched the horsemen trotting through the streets of the town and into the open country beyond. He gazed after them until all he could see was a tiny cloud of dust on the horizon. Then even that was gone.

The Emperor sighed heavily and moved away from the window. He had done all within his power for the sons of his favourite daughter. If they would use their own strength and courage and the two magic gifts, he knew they would find a proud destiny.

3 🌿

The City of the Dagger

The army of the two princes rolled across China and through the mountains of Yunan. As they moved on, into the unknown country beyond the frontier, the news of their coming flamed like a brushfire across the land. The thousands of horsemen and the great war-elephants struck fear into the hearts of the people along the way, and villagers fled in terror to take refuge in the forests and the hills.

The brothers left the army when they were still some distance from the Golden Cave and rode on ahead to see their mother, who had waited so long for their return.

Her joy at seeing them was almost more than she could bear. She spread a feast before them and listened hungrily to the tale of their adventures and to all they could tell her of her father and her sisters and the people of the court. Then she opened the rich gifts sent by the imperial family—chests of spices, rolls of rainbow-coloured silk, delicate carvings of jade and the finest porcelain.

Finally the boys showed their mother the dagger and the gong. When they told her of the Emperor's last words to them, her eyes filled with tears, but her voice was proud as she answered. "Go forth, my sons, and find your future kingdoms. I shall not be the one to hold you from your destiny."

So the two princes, with a last farewell, crossed the Irrawaddy River and joined their army for the march southwestward through the forest.

Each evening, when they camped for the night, the gong was beaten and the dagger thrown; and each evening the dagger fell flat upon the earth and the gong was mute.

They had travelled more than a hundred miles when suddenly the gong spoke. Its voice was astonishing for so small and poor an instrument. Men fell on their faces for fear as the evening air was filled with a tremendous booming sound that rolled around the hills and died away at last in deep rumblings like distant thunder.

Then, as though in answer, they heard the roar of a tiger. It seemed to come from the centre of the camp, yet no tiger could be seen. All night long they heard the roaring around them, as though the tiger were prowling within sight of their fires.

"The gong has spoken," said the elder brother, looking out over the camp in the morning. "Here I shall plant my capital city, at the centre of my kingdom, and it shall be called the City of the Tiger. Our travels together are ended, O my brother. May your dagger guide you to as fair a place as this!"

"Farewell," said the younger prince, "May you rule your land long and happily! Let the river be the boundary between us. I shall seek my kingdom on the other side." And gathering his army, the younger brother led them across the Irrawaddy and into the hilly country of the eastern bank.

Each evening, after the day's march was done, he threw down his dagger, and each evening it fell flat at his feet. How long, he wondered, must they travel through this dreary wilderness?

One day, weary and discouraged, they stopped to make camp in a bleak place among towering crags. The prince unsheathed the dagger and carelessly flung it down. He bent to pick it up, as he had done so many times before, and to his amazement he saw the bright blade standing upright and quivering in the stony soil.

In any other place he would have shouted aloud to break the news, but how could he build a city in this

terrible country? There was no water and no level ground for building or for growing crops. Here was a riddle that only his three wise counsellors could solve.

"O Prince," said the wisest one, "as I remember, the centre of your brother's realm was to be at the place where the gong sounded. The place where the dagger struck into the earth was not to be the centre of your land but somewhere within its borders. If we climb the height ahead of us, we may find a clue to the riddle."

So the prince and his three counsellors turned their backs on the setting sun and the river far below, and began to climb the eastern hill. The way was steep and they were tired, but when they reached the top, their hearts leaped up. Before them lay a vast plain, watered by another great river. Far away, yet clearly to be seen, the river split into two broad silver streams and flowed around a long narrow island.

"Look!" cried the prince. "We have our answer! Behold the dagger!"

The counsellors peered in the direction of his outflung arm, and in the light of the setting sun they saw what he had seen. The upper part of the river was shaped like the silver handle of the dagger. The two streams enclosing the island were the two edges of the dagger's shining blade.

When the army moved camp in the morning and set out for the plain, the earth in which the dagger still stood was carefully dug up and put into a locked casket. Eventually it was placed in the treasure chamber of a large pagoda in the centre of the prince's island city, which is known to this day as the City of the Dagger.

A palace was built for the prince in his new capital, and on the day he moved into the palace a golden umbrella, hung with tinkling silver bells, was placed on the top of the great pagoda. All the people feasted and rejoiced that day, and at night many awoke to hear the roars of a tiger circling the city. The prince listened with gladness in his heart, for he knew the voice of the tiger was a sign that all was well.

4

The Two Brides

Secure in his new city, the prince set out to enlarge his realm. Like his grandfather, he was a born warrior, and in a short time he had conquered broad lands around the City of the Dagger.

His armies seized rich farming land, splendid forests of teak and mines of rubies. They even overran the ruined city of Tagaung, an eery deserted place that had been the capital of Burma long ago.

When news of the capture of Tagaung reached the ears of the Burmese king, he was alarmed. He had no army ready to stand against the prince's footsoldiers, cavalry and war-elephants. Could there be some other, more peaceful, way to stop the conquests of the prince?

In his city of Pagan, the Burmese king summoned his ministers, wise men and astrologers. After careful thought they gave him the advice he needed, and in a few weeks a swift messenger was sent from Pagan to the City of the Dagger.

The prince was taking his ease in the palace when the messenger arrived. The man prostrated himself before the throne and in high-sounding and flattering terms he praised the prince's courage, wisdom and skill in war.

"The King of Burma, O Prince," said the messenger, "wishes to extend his friendship to you, who have shown yourself to be such a great warrior and wise ruler. As a token of his esteem, and to link himself with you in lasting alliance, he offers to you the hand of his daughter in marriage."

The prince was delighted, but his three counsellors were puzzled and deeply suspicious. Why should a powerful king, ruling over a country many times the size of the new state, make such an offer to a mere upstart princeling? They cautioned the prince to delay his answer, but he was impatient and had no wish to appear uncivil to the Burmese king. He declared at once that he was most grateful for the honour done to him, and he would be overjoyed to welcome the Burmese princess as his bride.

The Burmese messenger had hardly left the city when a courier from China came knocking at the palace gate. Ushered into the throne room, he bent low before the prince and handed him a letter from the Emperor.

"My grandson of the Magic Dagger," the Emperor wrote, "the wise men of my court, who can see into the future, warn me that you will fall into great danger, risking your life and your state, if you marry a foreigner. I am therefore sending you a princess worthy to be your bride. With this princess as your wife, you will be happy, healthy and successful, living long and reigning well. Be Warned."

The words struck like hammer-blows, and the prince bowed his head in dismay. Two brides were coming— one he had already sent for; the other was being sent to him. What was he to do? Could the Emperor's magicians, who had made the gong and the dagger, really see so far into the future? Yet to change his mind now and refuse the Burmese princess would be equal to a declaration of war. The Burmese king would be bound to wipe out the insult in blood. On the other hand it was unthinkable to reject the Chinese princess, sent to him by his grandfather. If he asked the advice of his counsellors, already so suspicious of the Burmese king, he knew they would press him to accept the Chinese princess. But how could he?

At last, in desperation, he summoned his most trusted officer and sent him on a difficult and lonely errand. After three weeks of hard riding, the man was back at the palace and bowing before the prince.

"Speak! have you seen them both?" the prince demanded.

"Indeed, I have, my lord."

"Then what are they like? Tell me quickly!"

"The Chinese princess," said the officer, choosing his words with care, "is a person of the utmost refinement. She must have been very beautiful when she was young. But sire, she cannot be less than forty-five years old."

"And what of the other princess?"

"Oh, sire, she is beautiful! You have only to look at her and you are enthralled. What a voice—so sweet to listen to! No, sire, in beauty there is no comparison between them. And the Burmese princess is but seventeen years of age."

At once the prince sent a company of courtiers, musicians and entertainers to meet the Chinese princess and her retinue. They showered her with gifts and made her journey gay with feasting and music. Yet to the princess the way seemed endless, much longer than she had been led to expect. The palanquin in which she rode seemed to be travelling in ever-widening circles, up and down the most terrifying slopes. One mountain path was so cruelly steep that it was remembered forever as the spot where the bearers cried out in anguish.

Long after they had struggled past this place, the weary princess arrived at a beautiful new palace in the mountains, where summers were never too hot nor winters too cold. And there, in loneliness and luxury, she was doomed to stay.

If the prince felt any remorse about the fate of the Chinese princess, he soon forgot her when he saw his Burmese bride. He knew he had made the right choice.

He and his princess were supremely happy. She was not only beautiful beyond belief, but she seemed to read his thoughts and always knew what to do to please him.

For a year they lived a life of delight. Then the princess grew strangely sad until all her gaiety was smothered under a deep melancholy. When the prince persuaded her to confess the cause, he laughed at her gloom.

"My little lotus," he exclaimed, "is that all you want? Of course we must observe the custom of your land. As a newly married couple, we will go at once to Pagan to pay our respects to your parents, and you shall take whatever presents you want for them."

Within a week the prince and princess had set out for the Burmese border, escorted by a large force of cavalry. They had not gone half way before they were met by messengers with a letter from the Burmese king. The king's words were plain and blunt.

"Do you come in peace," he wrote, "or do you come in war? My subjects have heard of your march southward with your army, and they are fleeing in their thousands. Please turn back if you must have your army with you. We will then excuse you from paying us a visit. But if you agree to come with a small bodyguard and a few of your ministers, we shall travel with all speed to meet you at Taungbyon, only three marches from your start. Please come in peace as our esteemed son-in-law."

The prince agreed with his counsellors that to go

without his army would be the act of a fool. They would have to turn back. The princess, full of joy an hour before, was stricken with grief and refused to be comforted.

"But cannot you understand, my sweet jasmine?" said the prince. "No king or prince or general will go into another ruler's land without an army to protect him."

"But that is because they go in fear," sobbed the princess. "Now we go to visit my dear father. There is no need to fear. We must trust him."

"This is not a private matter," he answered. "I must think of my people. For their sake I cannot take undue risks."

"Then we must go back!"

The princess hid her face from him, and her body shook with weeping. The prince could not bear to look at her, still less to take her back to the City of the Dagger. She might die of grief, and all his life he would curse himself as a coward.

He shouted to the leader of the bodyguard. "Bring fifty picked men," he commanded, "and summon my five chief ministers. The army will camp here and await our return. We go forward to Taungbyon!"

5

The Curse

The village of Taungbyon lay on the edge of a forest, and a camp had been set up for the Burmese king and his retinue in a clearing among the trees. A company of courtiers was waiting there to greet the prince and princess and their party. The honoured guests were asked to dismount from their horses and were led on foot to the jungle palace, a large building of bamboo and matting in the centre of the clearing.

As they entered the long hall within, the men of the bodyguard were ordered to surrender their arms. They tried to refuse but a word from the prince forced them to obey. The men were then made to stand in two rows, facing each other on either side of the hall. The Burmese king and queen, in their tall glittering crowns, sat on a raised platform at the far end.

The prince and princess, having left their bodyguard, advanced to a carpet in front of the dais, knelt down and bowed their heads to the floor in obeisance. Then, just as the prince raised his head, the king lunged forward. In a single swift movement he seized the prince by the hair and thrust the point of a short sword at his throat. At the same moment each one of the guardsmen and ministers lower down the hall found a Burmese soldier holding a dagger to his back.

"Listen, O Prince," said the King. "You have one chance to save your life! Take the oath I give you, swearing upon these scriptures of the Lord Buddha— and you shall live. Refuse and you shall die!"

With the sword-point pressing against his throat, the prince swore to renounce the best lands of his realm— the rich country along the Irrawaddy River, the ruby mines and the splendid forests of teak. He swore that he and his descendants would never take arms against the Burmese king. Finally, as punishment for invading Burmese territory, he accepted a terrible curse that would follow him and his descendants forever. Whenever an heir to his realm was born, the reigning prince would die at the moment of birth, and all true heirs would suffer from bad sight or hearing, stuttering speech or lameness.

To commemorate this terrible occasion two sets of figures were to be modelled in clay, taken from the earth of Burma and the earth of the young prince's realm. The figures would represent the Burmese king holding the prince by the hair and pointing the sword at his throat. One of the sculptured groups was to be placed in the treasure chamber of a pagoda to be built in Pagan, and the other in a new pagoda in the City of the Dagger.

Her duty done, the false princess crept softly away, not daring to look back at her defeated and dishonoured prince. She had been a tool in the cunning hands of the king and his ministers. An actress, chosen for her beauty and her skill, she had been trained by the chief ministers until she acted to perfection the part of the Burmese princess. At first, she was proud and delighted to play her part, but as the months went by, the task of deceiving the prince became unbearable. Now, at this moment of his agony, her hidden love for him overwhelmed her and she would have given her life to undo what she had done.

In her misery she fled into the forest unseen. She wandered far, not caring where she went. She was sheltered in a peasant's hut, and then, casting away her silken clothes and jewels, she joined a small band of nuns to fast and pray and seek release from sin. The king's men searched for her far and wide, to reward her for her service to the state, but she was never found.

The gay young prince returned to the City of the Dagger a broken man. Too late he understood how foolhardy he had been to reject the advice of his grandfather and send away the Chinese bride. Yet he still loved the false princess. His worst moment had come when he had looked for her help and comfort after swearing the oath and had found her gone. Even now he would have forgiven her and taken her back.

But he knew that for the good of his realm he must have an heir to inherit the throne. His counsellors chose a new bride for him and the prince dutifully married her. On the day that she bore him a son the prince was hunting in the forest five marches away from the City of the Dagger, believing he would thus be safe from the curse. But he died at the very moment of the birth.

The heir to the throne was clubfooted and limped all his life. He too died when his son was born. The new prince was afflicted with stuttering speech, and like his father, he did not live to see his son. The doomed princes had no chance to be good governors of their state. The City of the Dagger, and the whole realm, fell into decay and disorder, as the Burmese king had intended.

The same fate passed on from father to son for many years until a prince was born who was determined, from his boyhood, to break the power of the curse.

He himself had poor eyesight and was lame, but his spirit was undaunted. He studied ancient palmleaf manuscripts, to trace the history of the curse, and he consulted local medicine men, astrologers and wise Buddhist priests.

At last an astrologer of great renown was ready to give him advice. The prince must marry a wife who was not of royal blood, and their first child must be born beyond the borders of the state. The astrologer declared that the birth would be in three years' time when the prince was twenty-eight. He must therefore make gifts of

clothes and food to the monks of twenty-eight monasteries. He must pay for twenty-eight boys of needy
families to be trained as Buddhist priests, and as a
final deed of merit, he must buy live animals and birds
in the market—five times twenty-eight of them—and
give them their freedom.

All this the prince did.

He chose as his wife the daughter of a trader in
rubies, and in three years' time, when she was to bear a
child, he sent her away to her parents' home. Then he
went up to a palace in the hills to wait for news.

Day and night he waited, without food or sleep, while
twelve venerable monks chanted Buddhist scriptures,
filling the palace with a holy peace. When a barefoot
messenger brought news in the dark hours of the morning, the prince collapsed. But he was not dead, only in
a deep swoon. The hour of danger was past. His son was
born.

The little boy was a perfect child, his eyes bright and
his limbs strong and sturdy. His parents watched him
learn to walk like any healthy boy, and when he was old
enough to talk, his words came without the trace of a
stammer.

The young prince grew up to be brave and handsome.
Men said he might have been the double of his ancestor,
Princess Mimosa's younger son, who had founded the
City of the Dagger and suffered so terribly under the
curse.

The two pagodas, built to commemorate that prince's

shame, can still be seen. The one in Pagan is shining white with tiny bells tinkling from its golden umbrella as the light breeze plays upon them. The pagoda in the City of the Dagger was never crowned with a golden umbrella, and today it is overgrown with moss and ferns and its weatherworn stones are slowly crumbling to dust.

What the people of the city still remember, and speak about with awe, is the mighty roaring of tigers all around their town on the night the little prince was born and the ancient curse was broken.

The Pool

The Chindwin, one of the great rivers of Burma, has many moods and many faces.

The river is wide and placid as it slips past the low sandbanks of Monywa, and fierce and terrible in the whirlpools of Massein. Through the narrow channel above Sitthaung the waters move in a mysterious twilight under a canopy of evergreens, but all along the river's course there is no place so peaceful and serene as the jade-green pool at Natset.

The deep still waters lie at the foot of a black cliff and reflect the shining image of a tiny white pagoda on the clifftop, shaded by a giant banyan tree. A path along the shore links the pool to the village of Natset, nestling at a bend in the river. Village people often come that way, mostly young people in love, and this is the story they tell about the pool. . . .

147

Two hundred years ago, when there was no pagoda on the black cliff, two girls came running along the path to the pool. They were friends—Ma Khin Nu, the fisherman's daughter, and Ma Tin whose father was the village headman. Both of them were happy that day. They had made a morning offering of flowers at the village temple to celebrate their seventeenth birthdays, and they knew that Ma Tin's brother was soon coming home after four years away in the city.

The last stretch of the path was steep and rocky, and the girls arrived breathless in the clearing at the top. They rested under the little banyan tree at the brink of the cliff and looked down at the pool far below.

"What a beautiful place this is," said Ma Khin Nu. "I would like to live here always."

"But it would be so lonely!" said Ma Tin, and suddenly she grasped Nu by the arm. "Listen! What's that?"

There was a rustling among the trees behind the clearing. The girls jumped to their feet in fear and saw a young man stride into the open. He gave them a keen look and then came running to meet them.

"Sister Tin and Nu!" he cried. "I've come home!"

"Ko So Mya," said Ma Tin, pretending to be angry, "you have come too soon! We heard you were sailing here on a big ship and would arrive in two or three days. Why have you walked instead?"

"I was on a ship," he said. "It was a large paddy boat that ran aground on a sandbank. No one can move it till the rains come and the river rises. I couldn't wait!"

He turned to Ma Khin Nu who was standing quietly with her eyes cast down. "I am glad to see you, Nu," he said. "You have changed. You have grown tall since I went away. . . ."

She blushed, thinking how he too had grown. The boy she had known four years ago had become a man, strong and confident yet gentle. As they started down the path toward the village, a wave of happiness surged over her and she could not speak.

Two days later the excitement of Ko So Mya's return was forgotten, and the village was filled with hustle, bustle and shouting. A big sailing barge had been sighted on the river, flying the flag of the Governor of the Chindwin. By the time the craft was tied up at the village landing stage, Ma Tin's father and the elders of Natset were all dressed in their best and ready to pay their respects to the Governor.

They went aboard the barge and entered the large cabin where a stout man, fierce of eye and heavily moustached, was sitting on a velvet mattress. The callers sat before him on a carpet set with red-laquered boxes of betelnut, spittoons and trays of long cigars.

The Governor greeted his guests and addressed Ma Tin's father. "U Kyaw, what news of the eighteen villages in your charge?"

"All is quiet, Your Excellency," replied Kyaw. "The rice is harvested and the paddy to pay our taxes is ready for you to take away."

"That is well," said the Governor. "We shall load the

paddy tomorrow. I have brought my hunting dogs, and if the hunting is good, I may stay here a day or two."

U Kyaw kept silent while the other men talked of hunting. As a devout follower of the Lord Buddha, he knew it was wrong to kill. He did not speak again to the Governor until it was time for the men to go.

"My wife, Daw Su," he said, "requests Your Excellency and your officials to honour our house by sharing the midday meal with us tomorrow. We hope all the village headmen and elders will be there."

The Governor accepted the invitation with pleasure, and preparations for the feast began at once.

Daw Su, with the help of Ma Tin, Ma Khin Nu and other young women of the village worked for many hours on the food. She provided enough to feed a hundred and fifty guests, but if two hundred came, they would be able to eat their fill. The wooden floor of the long living room, covered with smooth cane matting, was set with twenty-five low round tables. A slightly larger table, placed on a carpet a little apart from the rest, was for the Governor and his party and their host, U Kyaw.

When all was ready on the great day the guests began to drift into the room and sit down on the floor at the tables. Young women and girls in white blouses and gaily-coloured skirts moved about silently and gracefully to see that everyone had what he needed. They brought bowls of water for the guests to rinse their hands before eating and, as the meal went on, they hurried to

refill the curry bowls, soup bowls, salad bowls and rice
dishes.

The Governor was enjoying himself. He ate noisily
with great relish while his quick eyes watched the
girls come and go. He discussed with his Chief of Police
which ones were the prettiest until his eyes settled on
Ma Khin Nu. She was serving at the Governor's table,
and presently she begged Ma Tin to come out with her
to the kitchen.

"I can't endure the Governor and the Chief of Police
staring at me," said Nu when the two girls were alone.
"Must I still attend to their table?"

"Yes, Nu, you must," said Ma Tin. "Otherwise the
Governor or my father would ask for you and want to
know what had happened. Come, it isn't so terrible!

You must get used to men looking at you!''

But Ma Khin Nu felt frightened and uneasy, and the meal seemed endless. When at last the Governor and his party had gone, she helped the other girls to clear the tables and then hurried home to her father's house, glad to be alone.

That evening, when Ma Tin's family were drinking tea after their meal, U Kyaw was summoned to see the Governor aboard the barge. Daw Su looked worried, but her husband assured her there could be nothing wrong. How could the Governor possibly be displeased after enjoying Daw Su's wonderful food?

U Kyaw was still away when Ma Tin's brother came in to speak to their mother. He wanted to be alone with her, but Ma Tin insisted on staying to hear what he said.

She glowed with pleasure when her brother spoke of Ma Khin Nu.

"She is so beautiful, Mother," he said, "and I have been fond of her since I was a child. The gay life of the city was nothing to me, for I longed for Ma Khin Nu. Seeing her again has filled me with a happiness I have never known before. I want her to be my wife. Please, Mother, will you ask her parents for her hand in marriage? This is urgent! Will you go to them tonight?"

"My son," answered Daw Su, "we knew you were fond of Ma Khin Nu, and I am glad you want to marry her. I shall do as you ask, as soon as I have told your father. Nu is a lovely girl, my son, and she will make you a good wife."

Ma Tin wanted to dance for joy, knowing that her brother and her best friend were soon to be man and wife. She went to bed, far too excited to sleep, and waited anxiously until she heard her father come into the living room next door. When her mother spoke to him in a low urgent voice, Ma Tin pressed her ear against the woven bamboo wall that separated the two rooms.

Her parents were arguing. "That's all very well," said her father, "but I have an official duty to perform. Had I known about our son and Ma Khin Nu before the Governor spoke to me, I would have told him at once that they were to be married. But now I have promised to speak to the girl's parents on the Governor's behalf. Ma Khin Nu is to be presented to the king. Think of it—

she will go to court and be made one of the king's wives! She will be a queen! This is her destiny. We cannot change it."

"But we must think of our son," said Daw Su. "Ko So Mya loves the girl. He will become a shadow of himself. The light will go out of his life—"

Ma Tin had heard enough. Leaving her parents still arguing, she woke her brother and warned him to be silent. Together they slipped out of the house and she told him of the Governor's plan.

The Governor, aboard his barge, was well pleased with what he had done. "That girl is truly beautiful," he said to the Chief of Police. "The king should be delighted with her, and my position in the royal favour will be far more secure. A gift from the wild country of the Chindwin as a mark of the people's love and respect for their king! That has a fine sound, has it not?"

The Chief of Police looked troubled. "I heard a rumour in the village," he said, "that the headman's son, Ko So Mya, is very fond of the girl. There is a chance that U Kyaw may warn his son of your intentions instead of carrying out your order."

"U Kyaw is an honest man," said the Governor, puffing on a long cheroot. "If the rumour is true, he would have told me about his son and the girl—"

"Perhaps so," said the Chief of Police, "but if he warns his son, the girl may slip through your fingers."

"We must take no risk of losing her," said the Governor in a tone of alarm. "Go to the fisherman's hut and see that she is there, on the pretence of giving her a message. Post some of your men to keep a secret watch around the hut. We must be sure that she stays safely at home through the night."

While the Governor was speaking, Ma Tin was trying desperately to persuade her brother and Ma Khin Nu to leave the village at once. She urged them to make for the house of her uncle at Kabaing, twenty miles away by river but only twelve by land. She wept with relief when they finally gave in to her pleading and set out along the river path. In a moment they had disappeared into the night.

Black clouds covered the sky, and the darkness along the path was terrible. The two had to grope their way as though they were blind. Ma Khin Nu was overcome with fear and remorse.

"Oh, Ko So Mya!" she sobbed. "What have I done? Where am I leading you? The Governor could arrest you at your uncle's house! You are putting your head into a noose. Let me go alone! I can hide myself until the Governor is gone and it is safe to go home. Please go back! Save your life and keep your people out of dreadful trouble!"

"There is no turning back," he said. "We shall be far away before the Governor discovers we are gone."

But as he spoke, they heard the sound of shouting in the village. Soon they could see flaming torches moving to and fro at the riverside, and then came the barking and yapping of hunting dogs on the trail.

Again Ma Khin Nu tried to tell Ko So Mya to leave her, but he only grasped her hand and pulled her along the path. They began to run, faster and faster, and the shouts and barking of the pursuers came nearer on the freshening wind.

Then suddenly Ma Khin Nu tripped and fell. His arm was around her to help her up, but her left ankle was twisted and would bear no weight. Again she pleaded with him to leave her, but his answer was to take her in his arms and carry her up the last steep slope to the clearing at the top of the cliff.

He put her down gently just as the moon broke forth from the windblown cloudbank. For the moment they forgot the sounds of close pursuit. They gazed at each other and knew at last what must be done.

There was a burst of shouting as the hunters saw the two on the clifftop in the bright light of the moon. The dogs had started up the last slope when the lovers knelt together at the edge of the cliff by the little banyan tree. They prayed that they might be forever united in love. Then they stood up, his right arm supporting her about the waist. Fearless now, she looked into his eyes and whispered, "Come."

The pursuers poured into the clearing, and the two moved forward as one and stepped over the edge of the cliff.

The tiny white pagoda, with its golden bells tinkling in the wind, stands as a memorial to the young lovers. Their ashes rest there, sheltered by the ancient banyan tree.

After two centuries Ma Khin Nu and Ko So Mya are remembered with affection, sorrow and respect, and for centuries to come they will not be forgotten. The village people say that two good spirits dwell forever in the peace and loveliness of the jade-green pool and the banyan tree, always ready to give their aid to troubled lovers who call on them for help.

The Wonderful Drum

1

Three Lazy Sons

Long ago, in the mountains of northern Burma, there lived a chieftain of the Shan people. This *Sawbwa*—as Shan chiefs are called—was a small and unimportant ruler, but in his heart he was a man of courage and pride.

He could not forget how the country of the Shans had been invaded by the Burmese many years ago. The Shans had been driven from the rich green plains and thrown back into the hills. His own small domain, called Maing-kwan, was in a remote mountain valley, and his over-lord was the Burmese governor of Mogaung, a place where the Shans had once been masters. The Sawbwa of Maingkwan was forced to pay tribute to the Gov-ernor, and this made him angry and defiant.

The greatest desire of the Sawbwa was to unite his people. His greatest sorrow was the laziness of his three sons, Ai Hsi, Ai Hsam and Ai Huk. He wanted them to set a good example of obedience and discipline, and all they would do was to enjoy themselves. At last the Sawbwa resolved to teach them a lesson.

He summoned them to come before him in the main room of his house. The evening was cool, and the Saw-bwa warmed himself before a wood fire that burned in a big earthenware saucer on the floor. The three boys came in quietly and sat down opposite to him, watching his stern face through the woodsmoke.

"The rains are long past," he said, "and it will soon be winter. Yet none of you has even chosen a stretch of hillside to be cleared of trees and cultivated for next year's crops. The clearing should have been finished by now. Instead, you have eaten, drunk and slept."

Ai Huk, the youngest and most talkative son, tried to break in, but his father silenced him. "Tomorrow," said the Sawbwa, "you will start clearing away the trees on Stag Hill. In a week the trees must be gone and the land ready for planting. You must start early. You will be wakened at the same hour as other workers. Now go and get what rest you can! If you fail in this work, I shall send you to labour with the slaves in the Amber Mines!"

The three boys left the house, stunned and silent, but as soon as they were beyond their father's hearing, Ai Huk burst out in anger. "This is unjust!" he exclaimed. "The task is impossible! It would take ten men to clear Stag Hill in seven days. I see no use in trying!"

"Useless or no," said Ai Hsu, the eldest, "we shall make a start tomorrow. Father is right to call us lazy, but you are the laziest. I shall see that you stay at work."

"We must work together as we have never worked before," said the middle brother, Ai Hsam. "Father means what he says about the Amber Mines. We would be fools to risk his displeasure!"

Next morning the three brothers were roused early. Grumbling and cursing, they collected the things they needed for a long day's work—ropes, food, and the large knives called *dahs*. Then they set out for Stag Hill.

All day they worked, chopping, hauling and piling up brush, until the evening shadows lengthened and they were almost too weary to move. The land they had cleared was only a small patch on the broad hillside, but they plodded home well pleased with their day.

It was so long since they had done any hard work that they were sore and aching when they dragged themselves to Stag Hill next morning. They trailed up the slope and then stared, open-mouthed.

"Where are those trees I cut down?" cried Ai Huk.

"Where are those bushes I dug up?" wailed Ai Hsam.

"This cannot be Stag Hill," said Ai Hsi. "We have come to the wrong place."

But they knew it was Stag Hill. They found their footprints in the soft earth, a length of rope they had forgotten, and the discarded banana leaves that had held their food. Yet every tree they had chopped down was upright, unhurt and rustling in the breeze, and every bush, was standing serenely in its place.

"Well, it's no use talking," said Ai Hsi. "We must work harder than ever to make up for the loss."

They worked all day with a grim fury. By the evening they had done far more than the day before, but they felt no joy or pride as they plodded home, only a terrible weariness.

The next morning they came to the foot of Stag Hill and stood in despair. "It cannot be true," said Ai Huk, almost in tears.

All the bushes and trees were once more back in their places. The forest was as thick and green and beautiful as when they had first set foot there.

The three brothers gathered their wits and decided what they must do. They worked less hard that day, and long before the usual time to stop, Ai Huk called to the others: "I am too tired to go on! I am going home. Are you coming?"

"Wait for me!" shouted Ai Hsam in a voice that could have been heard a mile away.

MT. LEBANON PUBLIC LIBRARY

"I'm coming too!" shouted Ai Hsi.

With jackets and ropes slung over their shoulders and knives in hand, they tramped down the hill, talking and laughing loudly. Then in the deep woods at the bottom they stopped. They hid their tools and crept back to the edge of the clearing where they had worked that day. Crouching behind a bush, they watched and waited.

Presently they heard the patter of feet, and into the clearing came a large grey monkey carrying a drum. He jumped on an old rotten tree stump, looked over the newly-cut trees and bushes and began to beat the drum. "Ho there!" he called out. "All fallen trees and bushes, get back to your places!"

The words were no sooner spoken than tree trunks sprang upright and bushes righted themselves. The air was filled with bits of bark, chips of wood, broken twigs and branches, flung about as though by a whirlwind. In the flicker of an eyelid every tree and bush was back in its place, its wounds healed and its leaves gently fluttering in the evening breeze.

With a yell of rage the three watchers sprang out of hiding and rushed at the monkey. Ai Hsi slipped on a banana leaf and fell headlong. Ai Hsam charged on to seize the animal, but it shot behind a tree, and instead of the monkey he grabbed the tree trunk with such force that he was stunned. Then Ai Huk dived at the monkey and clutched it by the hair of the neck. They rolled over and over on the ground, but the monkey broke loose. Leaping from tree to tree it vanished into the forest.

Ai Huk got to his feet, angry and disappointed. Then he found he was holding the monkey's drum. "Ai Hsi, Ai Hsam!" he shouted. "I have the drum—come quickly!"

They scrambled over to him and stared at the drum. It was old and shabby, carved out of plain dark wood with a drumhead of worn leather.

"Come," said Ai Huk. "Don't you see what we can do now?"

He ran down the hill with the others at his heels. When they reach the bottom, they turned to face the hill and Ai Huk began to beat the drum. "Ho there!" he called out. "All trees and bushes on Stag Hill, fall down!"

There was a mighty roaring and a storm of dust. The boys threw themselves flat on the ground that shook beneath them. When they dared to look again, every bush and every tree on the hill had fallen down.

"Our work is done!" shouted Ai Huk, dancing in circles. "Let's go home and sleep!"

"Wait a moment," said Ai Hsi, the eldest. "Have you no sense at all? We must go home at the usual time to-day, and come here again tomorrow and every day until the week is over. On no account must Father know that the drum has done our work."

And so it was. At the end of the week the Sawbwa was very pleased with what his sons had done. He loved them, in spite of their faults, and he had no wish to send them to the Amber Mines. Perhaps there was still hope, he thought, that they would grow into strong men and brave leaders of their people.

Still the drum was kept a secret. The boys agreed that Ai Huk, having captured the drum, should take charge of it. He put it in a safe place, ready to be used again when the season came for clearing the hillsides— or before then, if some greater need should arise.

2

The Strange Rebellion

A few months after the adventure on Stag Hill, an exhausted messenger came stumbling to the Governor's Palace at Mogaung. The man's body shone with sweat, the cotton *longyi* about his loins was torn and dirty and his eyes were wild. He demanded to see the governor at once; he would tell his news to no one else.

The Burmese governor was seated comfortably on a mat in the great hall of the palace, chewing betelnut and spitting the juice into a silver spittoon. He was annoyed at being disturbed, and when the messenger collapsed at his feet and babbled about a rebellion of the Shans, the governor decided the man was mad.

"This is utter nonsense," he said. "The Shans of Maingkwan are the most peaceful people in this part of the country. We have never had a rebellion here."

"But Your Excellency," said the messenger, "I have seen the Shans on the march—hundreds of them. They have raided and burned the villages in your lands—no one can stop them! My own village has been burned, Your Excellency!"

The Governor dismissed the man and called the head of the troops. "A force of five hundred soldiers must go out at once against these rebels," he said. "Send messengers throughout the length and breadth of the land to summon all men to report for military duty. We must have a large force to crush this rising before it is beyond control. But what I cannot understand," said the Governor to himself, "is how this rising began. The Shans of Maingkwan have always been such peaceful people. . . ."

As fresh soldiers and recruits poured into Mogaung, the news came that more and more rebels were joining the uprising of the Shans. By now they were said to be four thousand strong. The Governor congratulated himself on his foresight and quick action. When the rebels marched on Mogaung, he was ready for them. He rode out to meet them with a fine army, well trained, well armed and confident. How could those ragged upstarts stand against them?

The Governor was watching from a nearby ridge when the Burmese army charged into battle. Suddenly he saw his men waver, and then, like grass mown down by a great wind, they fell before the onrush of the Shans.

The Governor did not wait to see more. He spurred his horse and galloped back to Mogaung with his body-guard behind him. Fresh troops were sent out to defend the town, but none could stand against the Shans. The rebels swept over them and poured into Mogaung. The town was captured at the first assault, and the Governor, barely escaping in time, fled southward to beg for help from the King.

Within a few days the royal troops were on the march, men who had never been defeated in battle. They had orders to seize Mogaung, crush the rebels and make the leaders captive. The King and his ministers awaited news of victory. When the news came, they refused to believe it. The invincible Burmese army had been beaten and put to flight. The Shans were triumphant.

Ragged fugitives, the remnants of the magnificent army, came straggling home to tell their wretched story of defeat and dishonour. They said that the leaders of the Shans were three young men, sons of the Sawbwa of Maingkwan, and that the youngest of the three had set himself up as ruler of Mogaung. The boys had had no experience in warfare; there was no explaining the defeat of the Burmese army. Could it be that the stars were against them?

The King summoned his ministers, wise men and astrologers and demanded to know their opinion. They

sat down on the carpeted floor, and the Chief Astrologer considered the question carefully.

"Your Majesty," he said, "we have studied our books and the stars, and in truth there is no favourable sign to support a military venture. Every sign in the sky points to failure for the next eight months."

The King frowned and turned to the Chief Minister. "What have you to say?" he demanded.

"Only this, Your Majesty," the Chief Minister answered. "There is something strange about these victories won by the Shans. In each battle men say that our troops have *fallen down* on the battlefield and let the Shans sweep over them. Your Majesty, with your deep knowledge of military matters, will agree that this is most peculiar. Something is working for the Shans and against their enemies—"

"This we know!" said the King impatiently. "What do you suggest that we do about it? If we cannot win a victory on the battlefield, how can we crush the rising?"

"I suggest, Your Majesty," said the Chief Minister, "that the answer to the problem can only be found in the palace of the rebel ruler of Mogaung. Now the principal Sawbwa of the Shan States is Your Majesty's friend; he could speak with this young upstart in Mogaung and persuade him to send an ambassador to your court. We would then send a wise man to Mogaung in exchange—"

"So you would have us recognize this young upstart,"

said the King, "when he became ruler of Mogaung through rebellion. What wisdom is there in that? Soon we shall have a dozen rebellions on our hands! Any rebel can say then: 'The Burmese king is afraid. He dares not fight this Shan. He will recognize any rebel as ruler.'"

A tense silence followed the King's bitter words. The Chief Astrologer gave a discreet cough. "There is," he said, "no sign in the stars to suggest that there will soon be another rebellion, Your Majesty."

The Chief Minister ventured to speak. "Your Majesty, any ordinary rebellion can be easily crushed by your troops, unlike this peculiar rising of the Shans. This is a time to use more peaceful means of conquest, and if we dispatch an ambassador to Mogaung, a man of wisdom and understanding—"

"Very well," said the King. "Send for the Principal Sawbwa of the Shans. I will see him as soon as he arrives and arrange for an exchange of envoys with Mogaung."

The King came down from his throne, and as he walked across the room, the ministers and wise men and attendants lowered their heads to the floor until the sound of a closing door told them that the King had gone.

3

The King's Ambassador

Ai Huk, as the new ruler of Mogaung, was greatly flat-
tered when the principal Sawbwa of the Shans invited
him to visit his state. When his host suggested sending
an envoy from Mogaung to the Burmese court, to begin
a friendship instead of continuing the war, Ai Huk
readily agreed. In addition, he undertook to receive the
Burmese ambassador with proper respect and civility.

In due course an elderly gentleman from the Burmese court arrived in Mogaung. He was soberly dressed for a man of high office, but his retinue was brilliantly clad in silks and jewels. There were not only the Ambassador's servants and secretaries but singers, dancers and musicians of the greatest skill.

U Ponna, the Ambassador, quickly won the affection of the people of Mogaung by his gentle manners, his cheerfulness and desire to please. Wisdom in matters of state was only one of his gifts. He was a storyteller, a singer and a master of many musical instruments. He trained dancers in new dances, directed plays and brought the delights of Burmese court entertainment to the palace of Mogaung. For the young ruler and his brothers life had never been so pleasant, so full of music and colour and gaiety.

The Ambassador was always welcome in the palace. No one minded his exploring every corner of the place or finding his way into rooms that were seldom used. Only his questions about the Shans' extraordinary victories in the war brought a gentle rebuff from the young ruler. "The war is over," said Ai Huk, laughing. "Let us not speak of it! Have you a new play for us tonight?"

Weeks went by, and U Ponna was no nearer to discovering the secret of the Shans' victories. He knew the King would be growing impatient. The Shan ruler must be hiding a secret weapon, but what and where?

In the small hours of a sleepless night U Ponna considered what he would have done if he had such a

weapon to hide. "I would want my weapon at hand to combat sudden danger," he thought. "I would probably keep it in a high tower from which I could see any attack on the town."

He had already searched the eight towers that lined the walls about the palace and the gardens. The only other high vantage point was the many-tiered roof of the palace itself, crowned by a golden spire. On the lowest floor of the building, near the centre, were the royal apartments, but there were no stairs leading upward in any of these rooms. Then U Ponna remembered the long ante-room connecting the royal apartments to the northern end of the palace. This room had never been used during his weeks at Mogaung, and he resolved to explore it as a last hope.

His opportunity came a few days later when the Mogaung ruler and his family and the whole court were going to the dedication of a new monastery in the town. U Ponna pretended to be ill and stayed behind. As soon as the procession had departed, he slipped unnoticed into the northern room of the palace.

The room was empty, and there were no stairs to climb toward the roof. U Ponna began to tap the wooden walls until a panel in the corner gave forth a hollow sound. His hands quivered as he felt up and down the smooth polished surface of the panel. A knot in the wood seemed to yield to his touch; he pressed it, and lo and behold! a door at the corner opened noiselessly.

U Ponna's heart beat faster. He passed through the door, closed it behind him and climbed a spiral stairway to a little landing. Then came a series of long, straight ladders.

"I must be between the ceiling and the roof," he said to himself, panting for breath.

At last he reached a small platform with sloping sides. He was inside the golden pinnacle on the palace roof! In the middle of each wall was a handle. He gripped the nearest and pushed, and suddenly a hidden window opened before him. Cool air rushed in, and he found himself gazing out over miles of hill and valley, with the rooftops of the town far below. The new monastery, its courtyard filled with people, was in the foreground, and this made him close the opening very quickly for fear of being seen.

Without doubt, this place was the highest vantage point in the palace. He looked about the tiny chamber. The floor was bare, but hanging among the cobwebs above his head he saw an ancient drum.

 4

The Shans' Secret

When Ai Huk and his party returned from the new monastery, they inquired at once about the health of U Ponna. They were glad to hear that the ambassador was feeling much better.

After a few days' rest U Ponna was himself again and plunged into the planning of new entertainments. He was directing his troupe of actors in a play of his own composition when suddenly letters arrived from the Burmese king. Ai Huk was informed that U Ponna must leave Mogaung. The ambassador explained that he was needed for an urgent mission to Siam, and with deep regrets he begged leave to go the next day.

Ai Huk was stricken with sadness, and everyone grieved to see the last of U Ponna and his brilliant retinue. The palace became a dark and sombre place, as though the sun had set, never to rise again.

A month after U Ponna's departure, while the palace was still wrapped in gloom, messengers began to arrive at Mogaung. One after another, they brought news of an invasion by the Burmese army. Ai Huk roused himself and sent horsemen north and south, east and west, to summon the Shans to defend their newly-won country. The people came teaming to Mogaung, eager to fight. Ai Huk felt proud and confident, undisturbed by the news that the King himself would be leading the Burmese troops.

The Shan army appeared when the Burmese were within striking distance of Mogaung. Exactly eight months and one day after the Burmese king had consulted his Chief Minister, wise men and astrologers, the two armies faced each other on the battlefield. The ruler of Mogaung, with his two brothers and a small bodyguard on horseback, was waiting on a low hill. He was unarmed and carried in his hands the old worn drum that had served him so well. As his men charged down on the enemy, he raised the drum and beat it, shouting with all his strength: "Fall down, all ye Burmans!"

But instead of sounding, the drumhead burst. His hand broke through the tattered leather, and the drum fell to the ground.

The Burmese army, thousands strong, poured down on the Shans like a river in flood. The Shans broke ranks and fled. Ai Huk's horse swung around and carried him after his brothers and the fleeing bodyguard. They galloped for the hills and rode on without rest until they were far on the way to China. The ancient drum was left, broken and powerless, on the battlefield.

U Ponna had done his work well. With a sharp knife he had made many tiny slits around the leather drum-head. He had hidden the cuts by rubbing them with dust and then hung the drum again in its place in the golden pinnacle of the palace roof.

When U Ponna heard news of the victory at Mogaung, he sighed with a stab of sadness. He was glad to have served his king but sorry to have betrayed the proud young ruler, who had so much enjoyed the music and the dance.

The Chief Minister and the Astrologer felt nothing but satisfaction. The wisdom of their advice to the King had been fully demonstrated. Mogaung was in Burmese hands. The rebellion was crushed and its leaders had fled. Soon the Sawbwa of Maingkwan and his fellow chieftains would again be paying their tribute into the Royal Treasury. There would be no more strange uprisings of the Shans. Their secret weapon had been destroyed forever, and it was a relief to know that that mysterious weapon was nothing more than a wretched old drum, very much the worse for wear.

The Chinese Cure

 1

Prince Sao Hsi Han, the ruler of Mainkaing, was famous as a mighty hunter. His state was in the north, on the border of China, but his fame had spread as far south as the golden city of Pagan and the court of the Burmese king. His courage and good fortune in the chase had become a legend; and although he neglected his duties as ruler, his people loved and honoured him.

Then, one day, Sao Hsi Han returned from a hunting trip in the mountains to find his realm in deep distress.

183

His brother, Sao Hkun Khio, was a prisoner in China, many of his best warriors were dead, and the state was threatened with a Chinese invasion.

"I vow I shall give up hunting forever!" said the Prince, pacing up and down the great room of his palace. "If I had been here this would never have happened!"

The Chief Minister answered him in a low soothing voice. "The trouble began, Your Excellency, with your brother's ill-advised expedition to Yunan."

He went on to tell how Sao Hkun Khio had ridden forth with a force of two hundred picked warriors to attack a band of outlaws, who had crossed the border from the Chinese province of Yunan and were raiding villages in the Prince's realm.

Sao Hkun Khio had planned to trap the bandits in the mountains, but they slipped over the border into Yunan by a little-known pass. The Prince's brother and his men, close on their trail, galloped over the border after them, only to be caught in a narrow gorge and attacked by an army of many times their number. A mere handful of the two hundred escaped death and brought the news to Maingkaing. One of them had seen their wounded leader dragged away captive by the victorious Chinese.

Prince Sao Hsi Han stopped his pacing and stood with clenched fists. "This Chinese army," he said. "Were they disciplined fighters or only a rabble of bandits?"

"They were raggedly dressed like bandits, Your Highness," said the Chief Minister, "but they fought like soldiers."

"The Governor of Yunan must have planned this," said the Prince. "He has never forgotten how I defeated him three years ago. Assuredly he is waiting for me to invade Yunan to rescue my brother. . . ."

"Sire," said the Chief Minister, "before you take up arms, could you not try to rescue your brother by peaceful means? Do you remember your father's old friend Lee Pyin Yin, the mandarin at the court of the Emperor of China? It was he who settled your dispute with the Yunan governor three years ago—"

"To take up arms is the last thing I must do," said the Prince. "I had already thought of Lee Pyin Yin. I must seek him at once at the Emperor's court. If all goes well, I shall not be away for long. The Emperor is at his summer palace—a short journey from here compared with a trip to his palace at Peking."

The next morning the Prince set out with a small band of warriors, riding eastward toward the blood-red sunrise and the mountains of Yunan.

Once across the border they watched for bandits, but no man raised a hand against them. They rode through wild deserted valleys, climbed jagged ridges and forded mountain streams where the water tugged at their horses' legs and roared with the voice of dragons.

At last they came to the summer palace of the Emperor of China, cool and peaceful in its great gardens. The Prince inquired at once for Lee Pyin Yin and was

told, much to his surprise, that the mandarin was waiting to see him. A servant ushered him into a large
airy room, filled with evening sunshine. Lee Pyin Yin
was seated by the window, admiring a piece of carved
white jade, and he rose to meet the Prince with a gentle
smile.

"You are most welcome," he said, addressing the
Prince as *Sawbwagyi*, which means "Great Ruler."
"News of your coming was brought to me today by a
special messenger, but had you not come, I would have
come to you. I know something of your trouble, and
you may rest assured that if I can be of any help, I am
yours to command."

Sao Hsi Han bowed low, and then, in short quick
sentences, he described his brother's ill-fated expedition
and his own suspicions about the evil designs of the
Governor of Yunan.

"I beg you to tell me, Honoured Sir," said the
Prince, when his story was done, "can you help me to
rescue my brother from captivity—and possible death
—and my country from the threat of invasion?"

"Of course I can help you," answered the mandarin,
"if you, in your turn, will perform a service for the
Emperor."

"A service for the Emperor? What kind of service?"

The mandarin held up the piece of carved jade and
fondled it in his long thin fingers. "I know you understand," he said, "that your esteemed brother is in a
very difficult position. The Governor of Yunan is the

Emperor's nephew and a man of power. Your brother was captured in his province, having crossed the border with a band of soldiers, and the story of chasing bandits could easily be taken for a lie. . . ."

The mandarin raised his slender hand to silence the Prince's protest. "Perhaps you do not know," he said, "that the Emperor is gravely ill. Our cleverest physicians have tried to bring back his health and strength, but to no avail. Now, at last, an old doctor has discovered in ancient writings the recipe for a sure and certain cure. All the ingredients of the medicine are at hand, except the most important. These can be obtained only from the fresh-killed body of an animal so rare that few men have ever heard of it, and no man knows where it can be found.

"You, my dear *Sawbwa,* are the greatest hunter I know. If you can find and kill this beast and bring to the Emperor those parts of its body needed for the medicine, then the Emperor himself will give ear to your request for your brother's freedom and will guarantee the safety of your state."

"Oh, Honoured Sir," said the Prince. "I vowed to give up hunting after my absence brought disaster to my state, but now I shall be a hunter for one last time! I who have never failed to find my quarry will seek out this animal wherever it is to be found! And what of my brother? Will he be cared for while I am gone?"

"I shall have him brought here," said the mandarin. "He will be my guest."

"Then I shall hunt with a light heart and unworried mind," said the Prince. "Now tell me, Honoured Sir: what kind of beast is this that few men have seen or heard of?"

"You are weary and must rest before I tell you," said the mandarin, speaking gently as though the Prince were a small, impatient boy. "But I warn you that this chase will be no easy or lighthearted sport. You may find your last hunt to be the most dangerous and difficult of all."

 2

As soon as the Prince returned to Maingkaing, the news of his last hunt began to spread throughout the land, and there were wild rumours about the mysterious beast that was to be his quarry. None of the Prince's hunters and trackers had ever heard of the beast, and the Prince sent them far and wide in a desperate search for clues to the animal's whereabouts.

At last one of the men returned from a southward journey to the golden city of Pagan. There, in the capital of the Burmese king, he had met men who knew of the existence of the strange animal, although they had never seen it themselves.

Sao Hsi Han called together a party of thirty hunters and they set out for Pagan, with the Prince at their head. They travelled for many days, hardly pausing for food or sleep. When they reached the city beside the broad waters of the Irrawaddy River, the fabulous golden pagodas gleamed in the glow of the setting sun; but the Prince rode past them, looking neither to right nor left. He went straight to the royal palace, dismounted at the gate and requested an audience with the King.

In his jacket and baggy trousers of cream-coloured silk, stained with the dust and sweat of the journey, the Prince was an impressive figure. His voice was harsh and husky with thirst and weariness, and his eyes fiercely bright. The prim official at the gate stepped back in alarm and hurried away to see if an audience could be arranged.

Presently the Prince was summoned to the throne room. He strode in through the golden doors and knelt down to bow with his forehead to the floor.

The King sat upon his throne like a glittering gilded image. "Welcome to our court, Sawbwagyi," he said, in a tone of weariness and boredom. "I am told you have travelled far to come here. Pray what is your mission?"

"Your Majesty," said Sao Hsi Han, "I have come to beg for your help. I am a hunter and my quarry is the strangest and rarest animal known to man!"

The King's boredom changed to keen interest as he listened to the Prince's story and learned the reason for the hunt. "Your Majesty," said Sao Hsi Han, bowing low once more, "if I can only find and slay this animal that Lee Pyin Yin described to me, it may save the life of the Emperor of China, and my beloved brother will have his freedom!"

"Indeed this is a double errand of mercy," said the king, "and you shall have all the help we can give. My chief minister will send men throughout the city to find anyone who has seen or heard of this animal. But what kind of beast is it? What are its looks and habits?"

"It is strange beyond belief," answered Sao Hsi Han. "The animal's body is of great length and girth, protected by shields of iron-hard hide and supported by short legs. A thick horn sprouts upward from its snout. It is said to be more cunning than a fox and faster than a startled stag, and with greater strength and ferocity than a rogue elephant."

"To hunt such an animal will be a formidable task," said the King. "You are a brave man, Sawbwagyi. While we search for news of the beast, you shall be our guest at the palace."

He turned to the Chief Minister. "Please conduct our guest to the Lotus Lodge and be sure that the Sawbwagyi and his retinue have all that they need."

Sao Hsi Han had hoped for help from the Burmese king, but such kindness and royal hospitality robbed him of words. He bowed and withdrew, limp and tired but full of hope.

It was hard to wait for news, even for a day, and the Prince was already growing restless when the Chief Minister came to call on him the following afternoon.

"You are most fortunate, Sawbwagyi," the Minister said, "and I believe your mission is blessed by the spirits—the *nats*. The Governor of the Chindwin arrived here last night. I questioned him about the animal you are seeking, and he has heard that it roams the far northern part of his territory, beyond the country of the Naga headhunters.

"If you will dine with me tonight, you may speak with the Governor yourself, and if you wish it, he will help you to plan a hunting trip to his country."

 3

The pagoda spires of Pagan were glistening in the light of a new day when Sao Hsi Han went forth on his last hunt.

He and his hunters stood on the deck of a sailing ship that glided up the Irrawaddy River through the early morning mist. A second ship followed, bearing a troop of the King's soldiers as protection against raiders and headhunters, and each vessel towed a *lone-dwin*, a long graceful dugout with upturned prow and stern.

With a southerly breeze to swell their sails, the ships travelled upstream for four days until they came to the broad meeting of waters where the Chindwin River joined the Irrawaddy. Then, as they turned up the narrower channel of the Chindwin, the wind died and the vessels could be moved only by the strength of men. Some were ordered to go below and heave on the huge oars while others, on the deck above, set their shoulders to the long punting-poles.

The ships moved steadily upstream, but to Sao Hsi Han their progress seemed maddeningly slow. When they came to the gorges of the Upper Chindwin, wild and beautiful, the soldiers kept a constant watch, but the Prince had no thought for the danger of flying arrows or night raids by headhunters. He stared at the channel ahead. They were nearing the mouth of the Uyu River, and somewhere along its banks the animal he sought had been seen.

The Uyu was too small and shallow for the ships. The Prince and his thirty hunters and trackers embarked on the two lone-dwins, while the two large vessels anchored to wait for their return.

For most of the way the dugouts could be rowed or punted, but over shoals and rapids they had to be lifted and carried by the sweating, straining men. The Prince sent some of his hunters along the banks of the stream to look for unusual tracks. The jungle swarmed with game. Tigers were often seen and heard, and there were many elephants. Sao Hsi Han passed them by without a glance. From morning to night he crouched in his boat, taut as a stretched bowstring—watching, waiting and listening. He lost count of hours and days and fought grimly against the fear of failure.

Then, one evening at dusk, the low cry of a tracker sent the two boats hurrying to the shore with a splash of oars. The Prince was the first to leap onto the muddy bank. The tracker showed him where a large heavy animal had passed, leaving deep imprints in the mud, and the Prince knew his long search was over.

The evening light was too dim for hunting, but at dawn the next day Sao Hsi Han and a small party of men began to follow the tracks. For two hours they pushed through dense jungle. Then the forest thinned and the tracks went down a slope to a large open marsh. Hiding in the cover of the bushes, the Prince felt the wild drumming of his heart. His mouth was dry, his body drenched with sweat.

No more than a hundred yards away was the animal he had come so far to find. It stood belly-deep in mud and slush. A tiny bird was perched on the beast's ugly head and another on the broad back. The Prince could see the grey, armour-plated skin, the powerful snout, the thick uprising horn.

He forced himself to turn his eyes away and signalled to two men to keep watch. Then he led the others to a safe distance and sent them to look for more tracks, as clues to the animal's habits. They soon found what he wanted—a well-worn trail to the beast's sleeping place in the scrubby bush two miles away. The Prince hid himself beside the trail and settled down to wait until evening for the beast to pass by.

His hunters were strung out along the path, also watching and waiting. Hardly an hour had passed before one of them gave the soft call of a dove. The Prince stiffened and took a firmer grip on his crossbow. That cry meant that their quarry had started along the trail from the marsh.

Suddenly the beast was in sight. For all its size and weight it moved noiselessly along the narrow path. The crossbow was ready, the steel-tipped bolt set in its groove and the taut string drawn back. As the beast came nearer, the Prince slowly lifted the bow to shoulder height and waited until only thirty feet separated him from his quarry.

Then he pulled the trigger. Twang! the cord sent the bolt straight and true to its mark between neck and shoulder. For a moment the animal halted. Then it charged straight ahead to receive a second bolt as it went by. It spun in its tracks and charged at the hunter, but the Prince sprang aside behind a tree, and the animal crashed past him through the thickets.

His men came running down the trail. They listened to the crackle of breaking saplings and undergrowth as the beast plunged away in the jungle. Then the Prince set out in pursuit.

All day the hunters trailed the wounded animal until darkness fell and they were forced to stop for the night.

They picked up the tracks again at dawn, and not far from their campfire they found the place where the animal had rested. Large patches of blood, still wet upon the leaves, proved that its wounds were deep. The men pushed on with fresh eagerness, confident of victory.

Suddenly the whip-crack of snapping branches warned them to leap off the trail and throw themselves into the undergrowth. The great beast charged past them, back the way it had come, and then swung in a new direction down a steep stony slope.

Now the chase was fast and hard. The wounded animal led the hunters through the thickest jungle, up mountain ridges and down into deep gullies. But its mighty strength was failing. The trail was marked with blood, and there were more and more signs that the beast had stopped to rest and to shake off pestering flies. The tracks showed shorter strides and heavier gait.

Sao Hsi Han took the lead and ordered his men to keep back. He moved more slowly up the trail with only two hunters at his heels. The way led along the lip of a gorge, a narrow game path choked with undergrowth.

They rounded a bend, and suddenly the Prince felt, rather than saw, a huge dark mass thundering towards him. He flung his heavy spear with all his strength, leaped high and grabbed the branch of a tree. The spear bit deep into the neck. The animal swerved, lurched over the edge of the gorge and plunged, rolling and somersaulting in a landslide of stones and boulders, to the dry rocky riverbed far below.

When the Prince and his hunters climbed down into the gorge, they found the great beast lying dead at the bottom in a litter of broken stone.

 4

The Prince would take no rest in Pagan on his return from the Uyu River. He had with him the precious packages containing the animal's horn and parts of its body. These were the ingredients for the Emperor's cure and must be carried to China without delay. Sao Hsi Han stayed only to thank the Burmese king for his help and to present him with a piece of the animal's thick gray hide, trimmed around the edges with silver.

The King was delighted with the gift and the news of the successful hunt, and he questioned the Prince about the remote corner of the kingdom where the beast had been found. Then he gave Sao Hsi Han the swiftest horses for the journey north to Maingkaing.

Messengers galloped ahead of the hunting party, and by the time the Prince arrived in Maingkaing his people lined the road to welcome their Sawbwa with music, song and flowers. When the tired hunters reached the palace and slid from their horses, the first man to greet the Prince was his own lost brother, Sao Hkun Khio.

The Prince stared at him, unbelieving. "My brother!" he cried. "How did you come here? Have you won your freedom?"

"The Emperor sent me here with great pomp," answered Sao Hkun Khio; and as the brothers clasped hands, the old mandarin, Lee Pyin Yin, stepped forward bowing. The Prince returned the bow with joy, too dazed to speak.

"The Emperor now knows the truth," said the mandarin. "He knows that you are not to blame for the trouble with Yunan. He has such faith in your skill as a hunter that he commanded me to bring your brother here to await your triumphant return. We know his faith was justified. You have slain the beast, but have you brought what is needed for the Emperor's cure?"

In answer, Sao Hsi Han ordered his men to unload the bundles from the packhorses and carry them into the palace. The wrappings were swiftly torn away, revealing the heart, the liver and the gourd of dried blood; the animal's hoofs and horn and the shieldlike plates of its grey hide.

"Have I done right, Honourable Sir?" asked the Prince. "Is this well?"

"All is well indeed!" said the mandarin. "What you have brought is more precious than gold. The dried blood alone is beyond price. The learned doctors say that this blood, mixed with the juice of sugar cane will cure heart disease in a week. Mixed with a little honey it will cure disease of the lungs. The horn ground with goat's milk gives strength to the weak and makes old people young again. This day I shall send these things onward to the Emperor's palace, and you will win his everlasting gratitude!"

"But tell us of the hunt, Brother!" said Sao Hkun Khio. "How did you slay this terrible beast?"

The Prince picked up a handful of broken stones that had fallen from one of the opened packages. He rubbed and fingered them as he began his story, and when he told of finding the animal in the marsh, he set the stones on the table. A large one stood for the animal and small ones for the crouching hunters.

Sao Hkun Khio was hanging on every word of the tale, but the Prince had a curious feeling that the mandarin was not listening. He seemed to be staring fixedly at the stones. Was something wrong?

When the last word had been said and the mandarin

still sat silent, Sao Hkun Khio turned to him. "Is it not a wonderful story, Honourable Sir?" he cried.

"Not so wonderful as what I see before me," answered the mandarin, like a man in a trance. "Sao Hsi Han, *whence came those stones?*"

The Prince smiled. "They are reminders of my last hunt," he said. "I picked up these and some larger pieces in the stream bed where the animal lay dead. I saw many such stones in that place."

He held out one of them to the mandarin. Lee Pyin Yin took the stone in trembling fingers and spoke in a low voice, filled with wonder.

"This, my friend, is jade, the most precious of all stones. Like jade, this is heavy and hard and has that gracious coolness to the touch, which comes from the essence of clear mountain streams. It is fitting that this stone, of all things, should be the reminder of your last hunt, when you risked your life, not for the empty triumph of the chase, but for the lives of the Emperor and of your brother, and for the safety of your state.

"Jade is the stone of power and virtue and beauty everlasting. It belongs to the living and the dead, to the earth and the sky; and in jade dwell all the qualities I see in you—kindness and uprightness, wisdom and bravery and purity of heart."

He rubbed the smooth, water-worn stone, and as he held it up against the light, it gleamed translucent and alive with colour.

"I have seen and loved jade all my life," said the

mandarin, "but never have I seen a stone of this glorious green—the green of the kingfisher's wing. Long after we are dead and our deeds forgotten, men will touch the coolness of this jade and gaze upon its colour, and artists will carve it into shapes of wonder and delight. . . ."

And so it happened, as the wise old mandarin had said.

The Emperor was cured of his illness by the medicine from the body of the slain rhinoceros, and peace came to Yunan and to the realm of Prince Sao Hsi Han. But the everlasting memorial to the deeds of the great hunter was the wonderful green stone.

In years to come men went to search for the stone in the far-off country where the Prince had pursued his strange quarry. They gathered up green rocks of jade along the banks of the Uyu River below the wild Kachin Hills. They carried the jade to China to be cut and carved and polished by the finest craftsmen in the world; and to this day, men still cherish this stone of heaven, the glorious "kingfisher jade," that was discovered by Prince Sao Hsi Han when he went hunting for the last time.

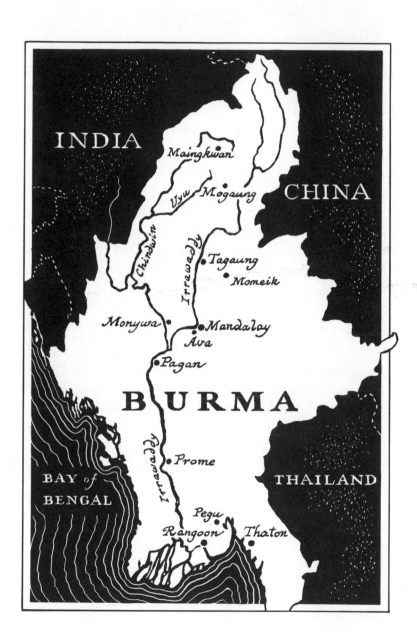

Historical
Note

Even the strangest legends often have a hard core of
fact. Most of the stories in this book grew up around
historical events, though some of the history reaches
back so far into the past that it cannot be dated with
any certainty.

Tagaung was founded by a prince from India some
seven or eight centuries before Christ. The kingdom was
destroyed, however, and lay in ruins until the fifth century B.C. Then, during the lifetime of Lord Buddha,
another Indian ruler came to Tagaung and gave the city
new life. It was this restored kingdom that Pauk Kyaing
gained, when he slew the dragon and unravelled the
riddle. In the early part of our own century a terrifying

ancient dragon, carved in wood, was still kept hidden in a cave at **Tagaung.**

Later in the fifth century B.C. Maha Thanbawa, the blind prince of Tagaung, established the kingdom of Prome and ruled there for six years. He was succeeded by his twin, Sula Thanbawa, who reigned five times as long and made Prome the centre of an important kingdom.

Ya-the-myo, the Town of the Hermit, was discovered not far from Prome by archaeologists about forty years ago. In that place Maha and Sula had left evidence of their love and respect for the venerable hermit who had foreseen their destiny. They had converted his humble house in the jungle into a monastery surrounded by a small town.

By 55 B.C., the year when Julius Caesar invaded Britain, the kingdom of Thaton was well known. Thaton had survived and prospered for over a thousand years when it was conquered by King Anawrahta of Pagan. The reign of Anawrahta brings us into the Middle Ages. He ascended the throne of Pagan in 1044 A.D., twenty-two years before the Norman conquest of England.

At the time of his accession, his kingdom consisted of a handful of districts in central Burma, but by 1066 Anawrahta had vastly enlarged his realm. He had conquered the Talaing kingdoms of Thaton and Pegu in the south and broken the power of the Shan kingdom of Pong in the north (called Mogaung in later days). He subdued the warlike rulers of the Shan States in the east, crossed the Chinese border into Yunan and even marched northwest into Bengal.

Anawrahta's reputation as a mighty warrior, victorious in many campaigns, may grow dim with the passing of time, but he will always be remembered as a great bene- factor, the saviour of his people. He worked for their good with boundless energy and enthusiasm. Above all, it was through his efforts that his people received as their faith one of the purest forms of Buddhism and had their language written down for the first time. Among the innumerable ruins scattered over the plain of Pagan the massive *Tripitaka-taik*, built to house the volumes of Buddhist scriptures, stands today as a fitting monument to this heroic king.

Anawrahta's son and successor, Sawlu, was murdered by his foster brother after a short and stormy reign. The usurper was then defeated in battle by Kyanzitha, who had played such a gallant part in Anawrahta's campaign against Thaton. The people of Pagan rejoiced when Kyanzitha ascended the Lion Throne. He had long been their hero, not only for his exploits in war but for his fortitude in facing trouble and misfortune before he was crowned king.

Building on the foundation of Anawrahta's conquests, Kyanzitha extended his rule over an area virtually equal to that of Burma today. Anawrahta had begun the golden age of Pagan, but it was Kyanzitha, in his long and glorious reign, who firmly established the city of five thousand temples as the capital of Burma. Pagan was

MT. LEBANON PUBLIC LIBRARY

the seat of the Burmese kings for more than two hundred years, until the city was conquered in the thirteenth century by the might of the Mongol Emperor of China, the dreaded Kublai Khan.

Yet even the Mongol invaders spared the temples of Pagan.

The Ananda pagoda, built there by Kyanzitha in the early twelfth century, is still a place of worship. The pagoda was a memorial to Kyanzitha's one great love, a simple village girl who gave him joy and comfort during a dark time of his life; and today, after more than eight hundred years, the splendour and loveliness of Ananda still gladden the hearts of all who come to Pagan.